"When I first got sick in high school, kids were pretty sympathetic, but the sicker I got and the more school I missed, the harder it was to keep up with the old crowd," Donovan explained. "Some of them tried to understand what I was going through, but unless you've been really sick . . ." He didn't finish the sentence.

"I've never been sick," Meg said, "but I really do know what you're talking about."

He tipped his head and looked into her eyes. "I believe you do."

ALSO AVAILABLE IN DELL LAUREL-LEAF BOOKS

FREEDOM BEYOND THE SEA, *Waldtraut Lewin*

GATHERING BLUE, *Lois Lowry*

HEAVEN EYES, *David Almond*

THE RANSOM OF MERCY CARTER, *Caroline B. Cooney*

PLAYING FOR KEEPS, *Joan Lowery Nixon*

GHOST BOY, *Iain Lawrence*

THE RAG AND BONE SHOP, *Robert Cormier*

SHADES OF SIMON GRAY, *Joyce McDonald*

WHEN ZACHARY BEAVER CAME TO TOWN,
   *Kimberly Willis Holt*

THE GADGET, *Paul Zindel*

# ONE LAST WISH

## Lurlene McDaniel

## Let Him Live

Published by
Dell Laurel-Leaf
an imprint of
Random House Children's Books
a division of Random House, Inc.
New York

**Visit us on the Web! www.randomhouse.com/teens**

**Educators and librarians, for a variety of teaching tools, visit us at
www.randomhouse.com/teachers**

**Visit Lurlene McDaniel's Web site! www.lurlenemcdaniel.com**

ISBN: 0-553-56067-0

RL: 5.0

Reprinted by arrangement with Bantam Books

Printed in the United States of America

First Dell Laurel-Leaf Edition March 2003

20  19  18  17  16  15  14  13  12

OPM

# Let Him Live

Let Him Live

# One

MEGAN CHARNELL WHIPPED her red convertible into the only empty parking space in the crowded parking garage at Washington Memorial Hospital. She screeched to a halt, grabbed her purse and notebook, and ran inside the glass doors. When she reached the elevator, she impatiently punched the button.

"Late, late, late," she muttered. Her first day on the job, and she was missing orientation. Her father wouldn't be pleased. She'd hit an unexpected traffic snarl. Usually, it didn't take this much time to come from her Virginia suburb to downtown Washington. If her car had wings she would have made it in plenty of time.

Meg pounded the elevator button until the door slid open. She barreled inside and hit the button for the fourth floor. It was her father's idea, not hers. She didn't want to become a candy striper for the summer. "Your therapist thinks getting involved will help you come to terms with what happened to Cindy. Maybe a job will be helpful," her father had insisted. Meg knew that her last choice would have been to work at the hospital, but here she was anyway. Part of her wanted to move on and connect to people, and yet she still grieved for her lost friend.

Meg had been overcome with grief at the news that her best friend had been killed in a car accident. She'd seen Cindy only weeks before the fatal crash. After Cindy and her family had moved away, Meg had been afraid their best friendship might end. But Cindy had promised, and so had Meg— "forever friends"—and they'd managed to stay as close as ever, even though they were no longer neighbors.

When Cindy's parents called Meg, she couldn't accept the reality of Cindy's death. Now, a year later, the therapist Meg had talked with felt she was ready to face new relationships with trust and courage. *Easy for everyone to say*, Meg thought, but she was nervous.

On the fourth floor, Meg raced out of the elevator and into the auditorium, grimacing as the door banged open. She was sure every person in the room looked up at her, including her father. He was standing on the stage, giving his opening remarks. Meg slunk into an empty seat in the shadowed depths and heaved a sigh. She mopped sweat from her forehead and wished with all her heart that she could be anyplace but here.

"As I was saying," Dr. Charnell continued, "volunteers like you, along with our faithful Pink Ladies, are a vital link to the welfare of our patients here at Memorial. The nurses are already overloaded with duties, so volunteers are necessary to enhance patient comfort. Without your helping hands and smiling faces, this place would be dreary indeed.

"For those who participated in our Saturday training program, you already know Mrs. Stanton, our volunteer coordinator." A woman with dark hair in a French knot waved from her chair beside the podium. "She'll have a few words to say, then she'll pass out floor assignments."

Others from the hospital staff spoke. When, at last, Mrs. Stanton wrapped up the orientation with an invitation for refreshments, Meg halfheartedly walked to a table piled with doughnuts and juice. Because she'd missed breakfast, she loaded a paper plate, then went to check for her name on the assignment sheet posted on the auditorium bulletin board.

"Hi. I remember you from the training sessions," said a tall, slim girl who was standing beside Meg. "I'm assigned to pediatrics. How about you?"

Meg found her name on the list. "Looks like I am too."

"I'm Alana Humphries." The girl smiled and

Meg felt she could like this person who seemed so friendly.

Meg smiled back. "Megan Charnell—but I prefer just plain Meg." She wiped powder-sugared fingers on her wrinkled pink-and-white pinafore, the uniform of the candy striper. "These stripes make me look like an overripe candy cane," Meg complained.

Alana laughed. "Charnell . . . Are you related to Dr. Charnell?"

Meg reddened. "My father." She hated people's knowing. She was certain they would think she was going to be given special favor, when in reality she loathed the whole idea.

Alana's eyes grew wide. "I think Dr. Charnell is the most wonderful man in the world."

"You do?"

"He helped save my brother's life."

"He did?"

"My brother, Lonnie, had a disease that was destroying his kidneys. He was on dialysis for years. Your father put Lonnie in Memorial's transplant program, and two years ago, Lonnie got a donor kidney. He's twenty now and doing fine. I guess my brother was really lucky. He got a transplant right away, which according to your dad, is highly unusual for African-Americans. It seems that organs are most compatible when the donor and recipient are of the same race, but not enough black people are signing up to be donors. That's really hurting black people who need organs." Meg had never really thought about such things.

Her dad was an accomplished surgeon who had taken over as head of the organ transplant unit at Memorial five years before. Meg couldn't count the times she'd heard the phone ring in the middle of the night for him. Neither could she recall one single holiday, one special family occasion that hadn't been interrupted by a call from the hospital because Dr. Franklin Charnell was needed to handle some emergency. For years, she believed that the hospital was his true home, and that his patients were his preferred family.

"I'm glad for your brother," Meg replied.

"That's why I signed up to be a candy striper," Alana explained. "To give something back. I mean, money couldn't buy Lonnie's life, so there's nothing I could give even if I was rich, which I'm not. The least I can do is volunteer to help out, try and make things easier for people who are sick like Lonnie used to be." She paused. "Did you sign up to work with your father?"

Meg couldn't admit the truth—she'd been made to sign up to help her pull out of a progressive depression. "Dad suggested it," she said, "and it sounded like an okay idea for the summer."

"Well, I think it's going to be fun work. And it's really cool to know I'll be working with you. I mean, Dr. Charnell's daughter . . ."

Meg squirmed under Alana's generous smile. How long before Alana discovered she was a fraud?

Her father came over, and Meg hoped he wouldn't mention her tardy entrance. "Hello,

Alana," he said. "Lonnie told me you'd be here. I
see you've met Megan."

"We were just discussing our assignments."

Meg nodded vigorously. "Pediatrics."

"I know. I asked Mrs. Stanton to put you there."

A warning bell sounded in Meg's head.

"Super," Alana said. "I really like kids."

"The floor's divided into units," Dr. Charnell
explained. "One for kids under twelve, one for
older kids. Both sections need extra hands."

"We'll do our best," Alana promised.

Meg only nodded.

"My office is in the same general area." His mo-
tives became clear to Meg. He wanted to keep an
eye on her, and she resented it. All at once, his
beeper went off. "That's me," he said. "I've got to
run."

Meg watched him hurry toward a house phone.

"He's so busy," Alana said.

"You've got that right," Meg replied, without
elaborating. She and Alana headed toward the elevator that would take them to pediatrics.

"I'd like to be a doctor someday," Alana told
her as they rode up to the seventh floor. "How
about you?"

"No way."

"You're kidding? I thought medicine would be
in your blood."

"I prefer doughnuts in my blood."

Alana giggled. "Honestly, girl, you're such a co-
median."

They emerged onto the pediatric floor. A huge

painted picture of a clown holding a sign that said "Kids World" adorned the wall. Meg paused to study the cute artwork.

"Get out of the way. You're in the middle of the drag strip!" a boy's voice called.

Meg flattened herself against the wall, turning in time to see a teenage boy pushing an IV stand with lines attached to the inside of his arm. He loped beside a very young boy who was rolling his wheelchair as hard as he could down the length of the hall.

Astounded, Meg watched them fly past with a clatter of metal and a cascade of laughter. *What have I gotten myself into?* she wondered. *What does Dad think he's doing?*

# Two

At the end of the hall, the boy with the IV stand halted. "You beat me, Mark," he said to the boy in the wheelchair.

The child grinned up at him. "I told you I could."

"How about best two out of three? Give me a day to rest, and we'll try it again tomorrow."

"You got it."

The older boy ruffled Mark's hair, and Meg watched him approach her, pushing his IV stand. "Sorry I yelled at you," he said. "I didn't want you to get mowed down. I'm Donovan Jacoby."

"Meg."

He glanced at Alana, and his eyes danced mischievously. "You two look like twins."

"Maybe it's the uniforms," Alana joked.

Donovan was tall and thin, with curling brown hair, gorgeous blue eyes, and a fabulous smile, but Meg saw that his skin had a yellow cast and that he appeared slightly stooped. He leaned against his IV stand. "Excuse my friend here, but we're very attached."

"Maybe you should be in your bed," Meg suggested nervously, after a quick smile at his joke.

"That's where I'm supposed to be, but it's pretty boring in my room. I was walking the hall looking for action when I saw Mark. Now, I've met you two, and things are really looking up."

"This is Dr. Charnell's daughter," Alana announced proudly.

Meg cringed inwardly.

"No lie?" Donovan asked. "He's awesome."

*My father?* Meg thought. "We're working here this summer," she said hastily, "and according to our training, we're supposed to help patients. Why don't I help you back to bed?"

"You do sound like your father," Donovan said. Yet, he didn't protest returning to his room.

Meg followed as he led the way, half afraid he'd keel over and she wouldn't know what to do.

"I'll meet you at the nurses' station," Alana called.

Donovan's room was sunny and bright. Although it contained two beds, only one looked as if it had been occupied. "Yours?" she asked.

"How did you guess? I lost my roommate last Friday."

Meg's heart squeezed. "Lost?"

Donovan saw her look of distress. "He went home."

She realized she'd been a doctor's daughter too long. In her father's world, "lost" meant died. "Can I help you?" she asked as Donovan climbed in the bed, trying to keep his IV lines from tangling.

"Can you hold the stand steady for me?"

She gripped the cold metal and parked it beside his bed. He lay back on the pillow, and she saw a flash of pain cross his face. "Should I call a nurse?"

"No. It'll pass. I—um—guess I overdid things."

Meg's training had taught her to be helpful and polite, but not personally involved. "Now that you're settled, I think I should be going," she said. "I haven't even officially reported in yet."

His hand reached out for hers. "Can you visit just a minute?"

"Maybe for just a minute." She found it difficult to say no. She glanced around at the bed, desk, windowsill, and curtain that separated his bed from the other one. She saw a child's drawings pinned to the curtain and taped to the bottom of the sill. There was a photo on the bedside table of a gap-toothed, brown-haired boy and a pretty woman with green eyes. "Your family?" she asked.

"My mom and my brother, Brett. Those are Brett's drawings all over the place. He's six and draws me a new picture for every day I'm in here." Meg's eyes grew wide. She began to quickly count the drawings. "Fifteen," Donovan said, as if reading her mind. "Where do you go to school?" he asked.

"Davis Academy. I just finished my sophomore year. And you?"

"Actually, I'm not from the Washington area. Mom and Brett and I lived in a small town on the border of Virginia and North Carolina. When I got sick last March, Mom was determined to find the best doctors possible for me. She sold our home and moved us here because Memorial has one of the best liver specialists in the country on staff. She's rented an apartment, but it's miles away, and she has to ride the bus just to visit me."

"You have something wrong with your liver?"

"You could say that. I had to drop out of school, but I would have been a senior if we'd stayed."

"Can't you be a senior here when school starts in the fall?"

"Maybe." He shrugged. "So, tell me, what's it like living with a doctor?"

It took Meg a moment to adjust to his shift in subjects. "It's like living with a god. Occasionally, Zeus comes down from Mount Olympus to mingle with us mere mortals." Her own candor shocked her. Why was she saying such a thing to a guy she didn't even know? She giggled nervously. "Just kidding. Dad's a pretty busy man, so sometimes it seems like he's hardly at home. How about your dad?" she asked. "Did he come with you?"

"My dad skipped out five years ago. Address unknown. There's only the three of us."

"He doesn't know you're sick?"

"No, but so what? Mom, Brett, and I are making out fine by ourselves. When this is all over with, maybe I'll look him up and tell him we made it without his help."

"I think I'd better go check in at the nurses' desk," she said, glancing at her watch.

"Sorry. I didn't mean to keep you so long."

"Want me to turn on the TV?"

"No, there's nothing worth watching."

Meg felt sorry for him and felt a silent tug-of-war with her conscience. "I'm scheduled to work until three. Maybe I can stop by later and see how you're doing," she finally told him.

"I'd like that. Mom doesn't come by with Brett until after six because she has to work."

She thought his eyes looked tired, and in the sunlight, his skin, as well as the whites of his eyes, looked quite yellow. "I'm not going to see you in the hall racing any more wheelchairs, am I?"

"Not today." A grimace of pain crossed his face, but he still managed one of his illuminating smiles. "No promises about tomorrow though."

Meg left Donovan and found her way to the nurses' station. At the desk, an older nurse, Mrs. Vasquez, said, "So, there you are. I've sent your partner on an errand, but I need both of you to help with activity time in the playroom for the children under age ten."

"I was with a patient named Donovan," Meg explained even though Mrs. Vasquez hadn't asked for an explanation.

"Alana told me. He's one nice kid. Has a friendly word for everybody and a special affinity for the smaller kids. We don't get many as nice as him."

Meg itched to ask more about him, but just then Alana came down the hall. "Mission accomplished," she told Mrs. Vasquez.

"Then it's to the playroom for both of you."

Inside the playroom, Meg discovered twelve kids ranging in ages from four to ten preparing for a session with an art therapist. Some were in wheelchairs, others were in casts, a few were bald. "From chemotherapy, I'll bet," Alana whispered.

Meg felt overwhelmed. She realized how isolated she'd been from her father's world. The hospital was like a separate city, with a hierarchy of people in charge. But in this city, people were sick, some of them sick enough to die. Seeing the children, small and vulnerable, carrying around basins in case they had to vomit, and with apparatuses attached to their arms or protruding from their chests, made Meg queasy. And it brought back the memory of Cindy much too vividly. Meg didn't see how she was going to last the summer in such an environment.

"You all right?" Alana asked. "You look a little green."

"Too many doughnuts," Meg mumbled. "Doesn't this bother you?" she asked.

"Lonnie was on dialysis so long, I got used to coming to the hospital. I saw lots of sick people. Now, I want to help them."

Meg wished she could feel the same way, but all she really wanted to do was go home. She began to think she'd made a mistake by agreeing to work at the hospital. She really wasn't up to the task. She made up her mind that at the end of the day, she'd tell her father that she couldn't manage it. That it was too painful for her emotionally.

At the end of her shift, she stopped by Donovan's room. He was sound asleep, and she didn't wake him. She studied his drawings from his brother carefully. There were many of a house with the words "Our Home" and "Where the Jacobys Live."

Nervously, she approached her father's office, where she discovered him hunched over his desk, doing paperwork. He looked up and beckoned her inside. "How was the first day?"

"I'm not so sure this is such a good idea for me," she said.

"Sit and tell me about it."

"I tried to help with activity time, but I didn't do a very good job. The art therapist had to help me more than the kids."

"You'll catch on."

She felt cowardly, wishing she could simply come out and tell him the truth. "I also met a boy named Donovan."

Her father nodded. "He's one sick kid."

"What's wrong with him? I know it's something to do with his liver."

"I'm afraid his liver's shot. That's really why he's here. His physician referred him to me because our program is his only hope."

Meg felt her hands turn clammy. "Your program?"

"Donovan needs a liver transplant. Without one, I'd say he has less than six months to live."

# Three

"DONOVAN'S GOING TO die? But he's not much older than me."

"He's almost eighteen, but age has nothing to do with it. He's in advanced stages of cirrhosis brought on by a non-A, non-B strain of hepatitis. Cirrhosis is deadly."

"How did he get such a thing?"

"His hepatitis is idiopathic." She looked perplexed, and her father added, "That's medical talk for 'We don't know how he got it.' Frankly, at this late stage, it doesn't matter."

"There must be some kind of medicine for it."

"I'm afraid not. And the virus has all but destroyed his liver. Sometimes, cirrhosis can be reversed, but not in Donovan's case. The liver filters out toxins—poisons. Once it begins to fail, toxins build up. Eventually, the liver atrophies altogether and the victim dies. The only hope is a transplant."

"Will he be able to get one?"

"Only if we can locate a compatible donor."

"What's that mean?" Meg's head began to swim with the complexity of Donovan's circumstances.

"A donor has to match in blood type, plus be about the same weight and height as the intended recipient. The liver is a large organ and can't be expected to function properly if it's mismatched. And there simply are not enough donor organs to go around to all the patients needing them."

"Why not?" Meg recalled how her dad would hurry off to perform surgery whenever an organ would be specially flown in for one of his patients. He was on virtual twenty-four-hour call.

"Ah, Meg," her father said with a sigh. "That's a complicated issue. To be of any use for transplantation, organs need to be free of disease and injury, so donors are most often healthy individuals who die unexpectedly and traumatically—often with a massive head injury. Anyway, families have to be approached about donation when their loved one is on life support, when he or she is declared brain dead. It's a very trying time for everybody, and families are in shock.

"It's not always easy for them to accept what's happened, much less agree to donate organs. Yet, people working with transplant services attempt to help families see that organ donation is sometimes the only positive thing to come out of such tragedies as premature death. The best way for a family to deal with the issue is to know how members of the family feel about donating their organs. That requires discussing it *before* a tragedy happens."

"Does Donovan know how sick he is?" Meg asked.

"His mother's aware of the gravity of his condition, but even though I've had several talks with him, I'm not sure he's totally accepting it. Kids, especially you teens, believe you're invincible, bigger than death. Also, the condition itself often brings on bouts of confusion and extreme fatigue that dulls a victim's perceptions about his illness."

*Had Cindy thought she was invincible?* Meg wondered. *Didn't everyone have the right to grow up and grow old?* "So, once you find him a donor, he'll be all right, won't he?"

Again, her father shook his head. "It doesn't always work that way. The transplantation operation and recovery period aside, he's not the only person here at Memorial awaiting a liver transplant. I have a list of patients."

"But you said he'd die without one."

"They'll all die without one."

Meg felt as if she'd wandered into a maze. "Still, there's hope, isn't there?"

"There's always hope. That's what keeps us going." His beeper sounded. "Excuse me." He picked up his phone and dialed his exchange.

Meg had grown to hate the sound of the beeper, and she felt particularly irritated now that she had so many questions about Donovan and his necessary liver transplant. She waited while her father carried on a clipped conversation and hung up. He stood. "Meg, tell your mom I won't be home this evening."

"What's wrong?" She looked up at him, watched as he removed his lab coat and slipped on his suit jacket.

"That was a colleague in Baltimore. He's got a donor heart for us, and I've got a thirty-three-year-old mother of two who desperately needs it. According to the National Network for Organ Sharing, the two of them are a match."

"Can't someone else go get it?"

"Time is critical, and I want the retrieval done properly. Nothing's more frustrating than having a perfectly suitable organ go bad because of improper surgical procedures or storage conditions. It's best if I use the hospital's private jet to go retrieve it myself."

"I'll tell Mom," she said. He was already out the door. Meg stood and shook off a chill. Images of her father, Donovan, and the hospital bombarded her, but the sound of the beeper took on a new meaning. One day, it might sound for Donovan. One day, it might mean medical science had located a donor liver for him. Still, she kept seeing the image of Cindy's face. For Cindy, there had been no hope, not with an organ transplant, not with hospitalization, not with any assortment of new and experimental drugs.

Meg hurried to the parking garage. All she

wanted to do was go home and put the entire day behind her. And also to forget what had happened to her very best friend.

At dinner that night, Meg shoved green beans and broiled chicken around on her plate. She didn't have much of an appetite. Her sister, Tracy, kept jabbering about her upcoming stay at gymnastic camp for the summer. Meg listened, half-heartedly, still brooding about Donovan.

"How was your first day as a volunteer? Do you like it?" Meg heard her mother ask.

"I'm around sick kids all day. What's fun about that?"

"Honey, it's good for you to be active, remember? You were getting too introspective, and your father and I were concerned about you."

*That's why it's called depression, Mom*, Meg felt like saying. The phone rang, and Tracy hopped up to answer it. She returned, saying, "Mom, it's Mrs. Hotchkiss from the Junior League."

Meg was relieved, knowing that her mother would get involved with her Junior League responsibilities and forget about delving into Meg's day.

Later, in her room, Meg flopped across the bed. She wondered if her father's effort to retrieve a donor heart and save a patient under his care had gone well. She thought about Donovan's need for someone to die so that he could live.

Meg got a sense that she was viewing some kind of low-budget horror film. Maintaining human parts and flying them around the country for use in dying people sounded so bizarre. But she was able to see the necessity for the process in a new light because a stranger named Donovan had become a real person, not a case.

Sadness engulfed her, and she tried to recall the last time she'd felt happy. Somehow, since the accident, she didn't feel right about being happy because Cindy could no longer be happy. Her therapist had helped her see that she had to overcome that feeling. She remembered the night Cindy had been with her for a sleep-over and it had been great.

*"So, what do you think, Meg? Will I always be the tallest girl in our class, or will my hormones give up and leave me in peace for a while?"*

Meg sat upright and looked around her room, half expecting Cindy to be sitting on the floor, complaining about her height. The room was empty. Of course, she'd imagined her friend's voice. "You're going to have sporadic periods of renewed grieving," Dr. Miller, her therapist, had often explained and tried to reassure her. "We call them 'grieving pangs,' and they're normal. It's when a person can't rise up out of the spiral and go on with everyday life that he or she gets into trouble."

Suddenly, Meg realized she was tired of feeling grieving pangs. Agitated, she circled her room. She didn't want to think about the loss of Cindy. She wanted to forget the pain. What could her father and Dr. Miller have been thinking to suggest that she work around sick people at the hospital? This wasn't going to help her. It was harming her.

Meg went to her desk and picked up Cindy's class photo. The image grinned out at her—a slim girl with a head of wild, frizzy brown hair and freckles on her face. "I wish you could meet this guy I saw today. Even though he's sick, he's cute. You'd probably think he was too thin, but that's not his fault. I wish ..." Meg's voice trailed.

She carefully set down the photograph. It was stupid to be talking to a picture. She glanced at the bedside clock. It was only nine o'clock, but she suddenly felt overwhelmed by exhaustion. "Excessive sleeping is a sign of depression," the therapist had informed Meg when she'd first started seeing her in April.

"So what?" Meg said to the memory of Dr. Miller's face. Without a second thought, she flipped off the light and crawled beneath the covers, into the blessed arms of a deep, forgetful sleep.

# Four

❧

WHEN MEG ARRIVED at the hospital the next morning, she headed straight to Donovan's room. Once there, she skidded to a halt, seeing a woman and a young boy beside Donovan's bed. "Meg," Donovan greeted her. "Come meet my mom and brother."

"Donovan's been talking about you," said the woman with hair the same color as her son's.

"He said you were pretty," the young boy blurted out. "You are, but I don't like girls very much. I think they're mean. Bonnie Oakland's mean. She's in my class, and she always butts in line and my teacher doesn't do anything about it."

"Brett, that's not polite," his mother scolded. "Excuse Mr. Chatterbox here. Today's teacher conference at his day school. I asked my boss if I could come in late so that I could meet with Brett's teacher." She patted Donovan's arm. "And on our way home, we stopped to see Donovan."

"Nice to meet you," Meg said, her mind still dwelling on Brett's comment about Donovan's thinking she was pretty. She'd struggled with her weight most of her life, and boys had never seemed to notice her the way they did slimmer girls.

"I'm glad you didn't go right home," Donovan told Meg. "I wanted you to meet each other."

"It's *not* home," Brett interrupted. "It's an apartment. And I hate it."

"It's home for now, big guy," Donovan said. "Come on and climb up on the bed with me. I've got something for you."

Eagerly, Brett scrambled up on the bed. Meg knew she should say something about its being against the rules for anyone other than a patient to be in the bed, but she couldn't bring herself to spoil the look of delight on Brett's face.

Donovan reached under his pillow and pulled out a toy laser gun. Brett's eyes grew large. "Wow. Thanks."

"Where'd you get that?" his mother asked.

"I coaxed one of the night-shift nurses into buying it for me." He offered his melting smile, and Meg realized that he could probably coax Eskimos into buying ice cubes. "Don't worry—I paid for it."

"But the money—"

"I've been saving what you give me." He ruffled Brett's hair, while the younger boy busily removed the packaging from the bright plastic pistol.

Meg noted that Mrs. Jacoby seemed genuinely concerned about the expense. Meg couldn't imagine not having enough money to buy a small toy.

"I only want you to have enough for the things you want and need for yourself," Mrs. Jacoby said.

"What I need, I can't buy," Donovan replied.

The expression on his mother's face tore at Meg's heart, and after Meg's conversation with her father, she understood exactly what Donovan meant. "Let me see that," Meg said, lifting Brett off the bed and bending down to examine the gun.

While she kept Brett occupied, Donovan and his mother had a low, quiet discussion. Minutes later, Mrs. Jacoby said, "We need to be going, Brett. They're expecting you at the day-care center."

"I *hate* that place."

"What's worse? The center or school?" Donovan asked, distracting Brett.

"School," the boy answered glumly.

"Then lucky you," Meg inserted. "No school today."

Brett looked thoughtful, and Mrs. Jacoby smiled warmly at Meg. "We can't get back until Sunday," Mrs. Jacoby told Donovan. "I get paid time and a half if I work on Saturday."

"No problem," Donovan assured her, but Meg could see he disliked being alone.

Once they were gone, even Meg felt the hollowness in the room. She could go to work, but Donovan was stuck with another long day to face by himself. "Do you like to read?" she asked. "I'm supposed to go to the hospital library and pick out books for the patients. Maybe I could choose something just for you."

"Reading's all right, but what I'd really like to do is get outside on the grounds."

"You can do that?"

"If someone takes me in a wheelchair." He made a face. "I hate being pushed around, but if it's the only way to get outdoors . . ."

"I could take you down after I finish my shift today."

"What happened to you yesterday? I thought you were coming by to see me?"

"I did, but you were asleep."

"You should have awakened me. Really. I hate sleeping in the daytime. That means I'm awake half the night. You know how long the nights can be around this place?"

"Twelve hours—same as the daytime?"

"Technically, that's true, but it feels like a hundred hours when you're alone with nothing to do and no one to talk to."

She didn't dare admit that she knew exactly what he was talking about. Her periods of excessive sleeping were often followed by bouts of sleeplessness. "I guess the nights can seem pretty long in this place."

A lab technician strolled through the doorway.

"Time for my bloodletting," Donovan said with a grimace.

Meg backed away as the tech put down the basket filled with syringes, swabs, and glass tubes for blood samples. "Doctor's orders," the tech said.

"I'll see you later," Meg promised, and slipped out of the room. She didn't want to watch needles poked into him.

At the nurses' station, Alana greeted her, and together they went over the schedule for the day's activities. "I'll do the bookmobile," Meg said. "I already know my way around the library downstairs."

"And I already promised Mrs. Vasquez I'd handle the afternoon reading time in the activity room," Alana said. "See you for lunch?"

"Sure thing," Meg said. But she never made it to lunch. The hospital library was so devoid of appealing books for kids that Meg called her mother and asked if she could go through some of the Junior League book donations stored in their basement.

At noon, Meg rushed home, rummaged through boxes and sacks earmarked for the store the Junior League ran to raise money for charity, and chose an armful of new reading material. She came across a set of *The Chronicles of Narnia* by C. S. Lewis and decided to offer them to Donovan. By the time she returned to the hospital, lunch was a memory.

The hospital librarian seemed delighted with the new books, but Meg had to promise to help her catalog them on Saturday before she'd put them out on loan.

The afternoon passed so quickly, Meg could scarcely believe it when Alana told her good-bye for the day. Meg remembered her promise to Donovan, checked out a wheelchair, and was on her way to his room when she met her father in the hall. He looked tired, but was freshly shaven, and she knew he'd probably ducked into the upstairs doctors' lounge for a shower and a change of clothes. "How's your heart patient?" she asked.

"The transplant went smoothly, and she's in intensive care now. The next forty-eight hours are critical. If she hangs on and doesn't have a serious rejection episode, I think she'll make it. I'm hoping we'll hit on the best combination of immune-suppressant drugs right off the bat." For the first time, he noticed the wheelchair. "Going for a stroll?"

"I promised Donovan I'd take him outside."

"That's nice of you. The nurses are so busy, we're always shorthanded. And the patients need these extra touches."

His approval pleased Meg more than she cared to admit. "Will he ever be well enough to go home and wait for his transplant?" she asked.

"We're trying to stabilize him. He's much better than he was when he checked in a week ago. Even if he does leave, he must stay close to the hospital. He'll wear a beeper so that we can page him if a suitable donor is found. Dr. Rosenthal, his primary physician, and I aren't ready to release him quite yet, but I will give him a pass."

"A pass?"

"I'll let him check out of the hospital for a few hours to go have some fun. Unfortunately, there's not too much for kids his age to do up here. Too bad his mother doesn't have a car. I'd release him for an afternoon to her care."

"I met her and Brett this morning." Meg hesitated, then asked what had been on her mind most of the day. "They don't have much money, do they?"

"No."

"Then how can they afford a liver transplant?"

"Money, or lack of it, isn't a criterion for transplant consideration. Need is. There're federal funding programs for those who can't afford a transplant. It's complicated, and the paperwork's a headache, but I saw to it that Donovan would be covered financially."

"*You* did?"

Her father gave her a tired smile. "Don't look so shocked. I do it frequently. I want to save him, Meg. I want him to get the transplant and live a long time. I want to save everybody who needs a new organ. Unfortunately, sometimes the money's easier to get than the organ." He squeezed her shoulder. "You'd better get going. I know Donovan well enough to know he's sitting on his bed, dressed and ready to get outdoors."

Megan hurried off to Donovan's room and went right in. "Notice anything different?" he asked. Donovan was wearing jeans, a shirt, and a baseball cap.

"You're a Braves fan?"

His smile lit up. "True, but also I've lost my lingering attachment to my IV." He held up his arms. "See—no lines." He scooted off the bed, but even though he tried to act as if all was well, she could see his unhealthy, sallow coloring and the slow, painful way he bent over. "Let's get out of here," he said. "This place depresses me."

Meg couldn't agree with him more.

# Five

WASHINGTON MEMORIAL HOSPITAL was a large complex, located near the Beltway, an expressway that circled DC. Gardens with winding paths had been created off a patio area next to the cafeteria in an attempt to build a more restful environment for patients and personnel. Shrubs, flowers, and gurgling fountains lent the area a serene, peaceful atmosphere, in spite of rush-hour traffic that moved beyond the complex.

As Meg pushed Donovan's wheelchair along one of the paths, she recalled how the gardens had been one of her mother's Junior League projects. Meg had been only ten at the time the League had raised the money to create them, but she could still remember the day the gardens had been dedicated. She and Cindy had raced throughout the looping trails, pretending they were lost in Alice's wonderland.

"You're quiet," Donovan said, interrupting her thoughts.

"Sorry. I was thinking how pretty it is here." She pushed aside memories of Cindy. "Do you like it?"

"Yes. There was a park near the house where I grew up in southern Virginia. When Brett was a baby, Mom and I would take him and have picnics on the grass in the summer. I used to play on a Little League team there. Why, that park was sort of the social center of our town. Everyone spent time there."

"You sound like you miss it."

"I miss everything about home."

"Brett sounds as if he misses it a lot too."

"The apartment is really small, and it's up on the fifth floor, so he can't just run outside and play with his friends the way he used to. Plus, Mom works such long hours. It's usually dark before her bus gets to our stop." He sighed and stretched back in the chair. "Everything's changed because of me."

Meg stopped pushing and walked around to the front of the chair. "It's not your fault you got sick," she said.

"I know that up here." He tapped the side of his head. "But why does it bother me so much down here?" He put his hand over his heart. "I used to get boiling mad about it, but I don't have the energy to be angry anymore."

Meg understood just what he was saying. Hadn't she been angry about what happened to Cindy after the shock had worn off? She still got angry sometimes. It was so unfair! "So, if you're not mad anymore, what are you?" she asked.

"Tired. And scared."

Meg remembered what her father had told her about Donovan's not realizing that he was dying. Had he figured it out? "Scared that I'll bump you into a tree while I'm pushing you?"

"You're not that bad a driver. No . . . I'm scared because I don't know what will become of Mom and Brett if something happens to me. All we have is each other. It's especially hard for Brett. He was just a baby when Dad left, and he looks to me to be his dad as well as his brother. Mom depends on me too."

Meg thought Donovan seemed too young to have so much responsibility on his shoulders. Although she had often resented her circumstances because of her dad's medical obligations, she had had two parents and a beautiful home to grow up in. And she'd been basically happy until Cindy . . . "What about your friends back home? Do you hear from them?" she asked abruptly.

"Not much. When I first got sick, in high school, kids were pretty sympathetic, but the sicker I got and the more school I missed, the harder it was to keep up with the old crowd. Some of them tried to understand what I was going through, but unless you've been really sick . . ." He didn't finish the sentence.

"I've never been sick," Meg said, "but I really do know what you're talking about."

He tipped his head and stared deeply into her eyes. "I believe you do."

She felt her face flush. Except for Dr. Miller, this was the closest she'd come to discussing her feelings of loneliness and of being outside life's mainstream. "I guess people get so involved with their own lives, they sometimes forget there's a whole world of people who don't quite fit in for one reason or another."

Donovan nodded. "You said it. Even my girl dumped me."

Meg felt a pinprick of jealousy over the girl he'd liked, whoever she was. "That was nasty of her."

He shrugged. "I guess it wasn't all her fault. I was pretty hard to live with when the doctors told me my liver was shot. I was rude and mean. I helped push her away."

Meg could remember acting hateful herself during the past several months. She even had stopped studying, and for the first time in her life, her grades plummeted. That had been another reason her parents had insisted she see a therapist. "What's the old saying? You only hurt the ones you love?" Meg said.

Donovan grinned. "I've heard that before. Truthfully, Lauren is better off without me. She started dating another guy right away, so I guess she thought so too."

"Maybe things will get back to normal for you after you have your transplant," Meg suggested.

"Maybe. Listen, I didn't mean to sit here having a pity party. I really appreciate your taking time to bring me outside."

"I don't mind listening, and besides, it's been fun seeing the gardens again. For the record, I don't think you're feeling overly sorry for yourself. What's happened to you hasn't been any picnic."

He reached out and plucked a flower from a nearby bush. "Don't ever have your liver crash. It leads to weirdness."

"Why do I get the feeling that you'd be weird even if your liver was healthy?"

"I guess I can't fool you." His eyes glowed, and for a moment, Meg saw him as he must have looked before he got sick. *A real heartbreaker*, she thought. "Here." He handed her the flower. "A token of my gratitude."

She accepted the flower and tucked it into a buttonhole on her uniform. "Do you know we've been out here for an hour?" she asked, glancing at her watch. "I'll bet they're bringing the supper trays to your floor by now. I'll take you back to your room."

"Are you trying to punish me?"

Meg laughed. "The food's not that bad."

"Why don't you try it sometime."

"Like when?"

"Like tonight."

Meg felt her heart beat a little faster. He seemed to like being with her. The notion pleased her immensely. "I can't tonight. My kid sister is leaving for gymnastic camp, and Mom wants me to come to the airport to see her off. Dad can't make it."

"No problem." He looked away, and Meg realized that he thought she was making up an excuse to put him off.

"How about Saturday?" She remembered that his mom couldn't come for a visit on Saturday.

"I thought you didn't work on Saturdays."

"I don't, but I promised the hospital librarian I'd help catalog some books. I could come see you when I finish. Maybe I could bring along some videos and we could order in a pizza. I have a car. I could pick one up and bring it back to the hospital whenever we get hungry. Can you eat pizza?"

"My doctor says there are no restrictions on my diet right now. I think he'd like me to gain some weight."

"You can have some of my weight," she said. "I've been looking for a place to dump it for years."

"I think you look terrific."

"I wasn't fishing for a compliment. Honest. It's just that being overweight is something I've always struggled with." Meg wished she hadn't brought it up. She didn't want him knowing how inadequate and inept she felt around guys her own age.

"You don't have to fish," he said. "I wouldn't have told you so if I didn't mean it."

Feeling inordinately pleased, Meg pushed him back to his room, chattering enthusiastically all the way. After making sure he was settled and comfortable, she gave him the C. S. Lewis books. "Until Saturday," she said, and hurried home to put her sister on a plane for gymnastic camp. More than ever, she wished she could call Cindy and talk to her, but of course, that was impossible.

"You're certainly dressed up just to help in the hospital library," Meg's mother said as Megan started out the door early Saturday morning.

Meg felt her cheeks turning red. "I'm sick of wearing my uniform. Can't I wear something different for a change?"

"I'm not complaining," her mother added hastily. "I think you look nice. It's good to see you take an interest in your looks again."

Meg wondered if she should go change. If her mother thought she looked nice, maybe she had overdressed. She had wanted to look good for Donovan, wanted his approval. "I'll be at the hospital until tonight if you want me," Meg told her mother, then hurried out the door.

At the hospital library, Meg worked quickly while the librarian talked about how much she appreciated Meg's extra effort. She seemed so grateful that Meg promised to bring in more books and help on other Saturdays. Meg began to realize just how valuable volunteer help was to the place, and was sorry she'd resisted the idea of volunteering when her father had first mentioned it.

It was noon when she got to Donovan's room. He was dressed and sitting in a chair, flipping through TV channels. "I've got two games, a deck of cards, and a video for us," she said, breezing into his room. "What's your pleasure?"

He clicked off the set with the remote control device and turned toward her. "Can you get me a wheelchair and take me outside?" He sounded distracted and preoccupied.

"Sure, if that's what you want. Why?"

"Please, just do it. Do it right now."

# Six

MEG GOT THE wheelchair, and Donovan climbed in it, clutching a small leather shaving kit in his lap. "Am I taking you out for a shave and a haircut?" she asked, trying to joke with him. He looked tense and nervous.

"We'll talk outside," he said.

Bewildered, she pushed him down the corridor, into the elevator, and out into the garden area. The sun beat down, wrapping the afternoon in a blanket of humid summer heat. Many other patients and their visitors were out too, and finding a spot alone was difficult, but Meg finally parked the wheelchair beneath a willow tree that was off the beaten path. The tree's filmy leaves grazed a pond, where dragonflies flitted above the motionless water.

"I think this is as alone as we can get today," Meg said. She settled herself at the foot of his chair and gazed up at him anxiously. "Want to tell me what's going on?"

Donovan fingered the leather kit and glanced about. "I . . . um . . . guess I must be acting pretty strange."

"Not at all. How exciting can games and a video movie be to a guy who has a death grip on his shaving kit?"

For the first time since she'd seen him that day, a smile appeared at the corners of his mouth. "Now that we're out here, I'm not sure where to start."

"Start at the beginning. Take your time, we're in no hurry."

"I admit I've been hogging your time," Donovan said. "I'll bet you've got other things to do on Saturdays. I don't mean to crowd you or put something on you you might not want."

"I don't mind," Meg said, suddenly realizing that it was true. How had she become so involved with him in so brief a time? Yet, she knew that she had. "I feel like I've known you for ages."

"It's a phenomenon," he remarked.

"What is?"

"The way sickness makes you close to people you'd never meet or be with in the regular world."

Had Donovan felt the uniqueness of their relationship too? Had he sensed the curious bonding that had seemed to sweep away barriers of awkwardness that usually accompanied the initial stages getting to know someone?

"Your dad calls the phenomenon 'intimate strangers,'" Donovan said. "He says that people will tell a stranger sitting next to them on an airplane the secrets of their soul, when they won't tell their closest family member the same thing."

"'Intimate strangers' . . . interesting," Meg said.

"It explained some things to me. You see, I had a roommate in the hospital back in my hometown, and I talked to him about everything. He was what the guys in my school would classify as a nerd, but he was sick also, and we got real close over the weeks we were hospitalized together."

"What happened to him?"

"He got well and left the hospital. He came to visit me, but over time, the bond between us weakened. Maybe I was jealous because he got well and I didn't. Maybe it was because we never had a true friendship, just the intimate stranger business." Donovan shook his head, as if to clear out the memories.

"So, is that what we are?" Meg asked. "Intimate strangers? When you're well, will you forget all about me?" Meg couldn't believe she'd ever forget him.

"I think we're friends, don't you?" A smile lit up his face, causing Meg's heart to skip. She hadn't had a really close friend since Cindy. "Because if we're friends—and not strangers—I can tell you something and make it our secret."

"Is it something to do with your transplant?"

Meg was genuinely puzzled by the odd direction of his conversation.

"In a way."

"What is it? Have they found you a donor?"

"If they had, I'd be throwing a party. No . . . it's something else." He chewed his bottom lip. "It has something to do with your father in a round-about way."

"My father?"

"I'm confusing you." He raked his hand through his hair. "It's just that I want to tell you something . . . show something to you . . . that might affect our friendship. I mean, once you see it, you might have to tell your father about it."

"I won't if you don't want me to. Doctors are asked to keep confidences all the time. My dad will understand."

Donovan appeared hesitant for a moment longer, then he zipped open his shaving kit and pulled out a folded envelope. "I can't keep this a secret any longer. If I do, I'll bust. I'm going to trust you to keep it between us." He thrust the envelope at her. "Read this. I woke up yesterday morning with it on my pillow and not a clue as to how it got there."

Gingerly, Meg took the envelope. Donovan's name had been written on the front in beautiful, flowing calligraphy. Red sealing wax, stamped with the initials OLW and broken when the envelope had been opened, covered the flap. She pulled out a handsome calligraphed letter and began to read.

*Dear Donovan,*

*You don't know me, but I know about you, and because I do, I want to give you a special gift. Accompanying this letter is a certified check, my gift to you with no strings attached to spend on anything you want. No one knows about this gift except you, and you are free to tell anyone you want.*

*Who I am isn't really important, only that you and I have much in common. Through no fault of our own, we have endured pain and isolation and have spent many days in a hospital feeling lonely and scared. I hoped for a miracle, but most of all, I hoped for someone to truly understand what I was going through.*

*I can't make you live longer. I can't stop you from hurting, but I can give you one wish, as someone did for me. My wish helped me find purpose, faith, and courage.*

*Friendship reaches beyond time, and the true miracle is in giving, not receiving. Use my gift to fulfill your wish.*

*Your Forever Friend,*

*JWC*

Meg didn't know what to say. Blankly, she looked up at him.

"There's more," he said, reaching into the kit

again. He pulled out another piece of folded paper and handed it to Meg.

She unfolded it and saw that it was a check made out to Donovan Jacoby in the sum of one hundred thousand dollars. It was signed, "Richard Holloway, Esq., Administrator, One Last Wish Foundation." Meg gaped.

"Do you think it's legit?" Donovan asked. "Do you know anything at all about this foundation?"

"I've never heard of it." Meg racked her brain for the names of the charitable organizations that supported the hospital. "Money usually comes to the hospital, not to any individual in the hospital. Especially not a patient." She held the check up to the sun, but saw only a watermark for a bank in Boston, Massachusetts. "Do you know anyone with the initials JWC?"

"I've been thinking all morning, and the only person that comes to mind is a guy in my school named Jed Calloway—I don't know his middle initial. But it couldn't be him. He's poor as dirt and not very charitable either. No, it can't be Jed."

"How about this Richard Holloway?"

"Never heard of the guy. What's that E-s-q mean? Do you know?"

Meg puckered her brow. "I've seen it in old books. It's an abbreviation for 'esquire,' an old-fashioned term for a lawyer. I guess he's in charge of this foundation. Maybe he's in the phone book—we could look and see."

Donovan moistened his lips. "It's a lot of money, isn't it?"

"We both know that it is. Why would someone give it to you?"

"I don't know. All the letter says is that this JWC understands what I'm going through and wants me to spend it on something I really want."

"So, what do you want?"

"A new liver." He gave a mirthless laugh. "But we both know I can't buy one of those."

"There must be something else."

"There're lots of something elses. I have to think about it. I can't blow this much cash on myself."

"I think that's what JWC wants you to do with it."

He glanced off toward the willow tree. "There's another problem," he said slowly.

"Tell me."

"It—it's hard for me to say it."

"You can tell me." Meg felt her pulse throbbing in her throat.

"It's the part that involves your father," he said.

"How is my dad involved?"

"I'm afraid if he knows about the money, he'll take it away from me."

# Seven

"Take it away? My dad wouldn't do that!" Meg was both startled and hurt by Donovan's suggestion.

"I don't mean he'd take it away on purpose. But he might *have* to take it away."

"But why? Obviously, JWC wants *you* to have it." Donovan shrugged, and Meg could tell he was having trouble putting what he wanted to say into words. She tried to make it easier by rising up on her knees and clasping his hand. "It's *your* money. Why would my dad want it?"

He touched his other hand to her hair, smoothing it back. Her scalp tingled from his touch. "My family's poor, Meg. I know we're a charity case for this hospital. Mom explained how your father got us on Medicare in order to help pay for all of this."

"Money's not supposed to decide who gets organs." She recalled her conversation with her father, and how he assured her that need was the main factor in determining who got organs for transplantation.

"I know that, but now that I have money, will I have to use it for the operation?"

Meg couldn't answer his question. "What if you did? Would it mean you'd give up the chance to get the transplant?"

He stared down at the check. "It's a lot of money, and my family could use it for lots of things."

"How can you consider using it on anything else? I know your mother would spend every cent on keeping you alive. What difference does it make if it has to be spent on your transplant?"

"It makes a difference to me," Donovan said quietly. "That's why I'm holding you to your promise to keep it a secret from your father. If it's really my money, I should decide on how I spend it."

"But—"

"You promised," Donovan interrupted. He softened his words by stroking her cheek. "Friends keep promises to friends. That's a fact." He tugged her upward. "Come on. I think I can beat you in Monopoly. Want to give me a chance?"

Meg wanted to discuss the One Last Wish money some more. "But, Donovan—"

"Maybe I shouldn't have told you. I don't mean to put you in a tough place. I just need some time to think it through."

"I'm glad you told me, but I don't know how to help you with it."

"Then let's go inside and talk about it later. Right now, I want to have some of that fun you promised me."

Meg spent the rest of the afternoon and evening with Donovan, playing board games and watching the video movie in the recreation room. Several of the younger kids joined them, and Meg saw how fond they were of Donovan. He had a way with them, a friendly, open manner that put people at ease. She knew she felt comfortable with him.

By the end of the day, Donovan was completely worn out and couldn't eat the pizza Meg brought to his room. "You don't mind?" he asked as he crawled into his bed.

"Who needs the calories?" She kept her question light, as she shoved the unopened box to the side and fluffed his pillow. His coloring, which looked more yellow than it had that morning, bothered her. "Maybe you pushed too hard today," she observed.

"I wouldn't have traded today for anything. I really appreciate your spending your free time with me. It meant a lot."

"I had fun." Meg meant it. The time she'd spent with him had seemed to fly. "Your mom and Brett will come by tomorrow, and then it'll be Monday again and the start of a brand-new week."

"Another week in paradise," he mumbled cynically. His eyelids looked heavy, and Meg watched them close. "Don't forget your promise," he whispered.

"I won't forget," she said. He was asleep instantly, but Meg couldn't bring herself to leave. His breathing sounded shallow, and she was concerned about him. She wished her father were there to assure her that Donovan was all right. She fiddled with the bedcovers, smoothing them the way she'd been taught during her candy striper training. She kept thinking about the letter he had received, and the check.

Meg realized that she had been raised quite differently from Donovan. She'd been given many material things and had never truly wanted for anything. At sixteen, she attended a top private school, wore expensive clothes, had her own car. Not that her parents hadn't taught her values. Many a time, her mother had lectured, "We have a duty to help others who are less fortunate. Your father's profession is aimed toward helping and healing. I work hard with my charities because it gives me a deep sense of satisfaction to know I'm doing something useful for others."

Until now, Meg hadn't paid much attention. But JWC's generous gift to a person he or she claimed to not even know, caused Meg to pause and reevaluate her parents' philosophy of life. Why would a complete stranger give Donovan so

much money? Who was this JWC anyway? Meg
found herself not only curious, but also a little
jealous. Not that she didn't want Donovan to
have the money—she did. The money didn't
threaten Meg at all. It was the caring, the concern,
from an anonymous, faceless person that intimi-
dated her.

*"Don't pout. It won't help."* Meg heard Cindy's
voice in the back of her mind.

"But you don't understand. My dad thinks
more of his patients than he does of me!" Meg recalled wailing to her friend the day she'd gradu-
ated from eighth grade and an emergency had
made him miss the ceremony.

"Doctors don't belong to just their families,
Meggie. They belong to everybody," Cindy commented. "Sort of like the President, I think. I'll bet
he feels he owes something to the people he takes
care of."

"Then why did my father even bother to have a
family? Why didn't he just devote himself to hu-
manity and forget about having us?"

"Probably because he wanted you," Cindy answered. "Who says you can't have both?"

Now, years later, standing next to Donovan's
hospital bed, watching his chest rise and fall with
labored breathing, Meg recalled the conversation
with vivid clarity. Did JWC feel he or she *owed*
something to the sick and dying? Was that the
motivation behind the One Last Wish Foundation? And if so, where did that kind of compas-

sion come from? Did Meg have it within herself to feel the same way? The way her parents did?

She longed to talk it over with Cindy. Her best friend would have helped her make sense of it. But, of course, there was no Cindy. Stricken, feeling more depressed than she had in weeks, Meg pushed away from Donovan's bed and quickly left the hospital.

"Your father and I are going to run out to the country club and play a few rounds of golf. Want to come along?" Meg's mother asked her Sunday afternoon.

"Not really." Meg felt listless, as if her energy had been drained away. "I'd rather lie here by the pool."

"If that's what you want." She saw her mother hesitate. "Is everything okay with you?"

"Things are fine."

"You seem to be a little down today. And last week, you seemed so much more animated. Did something happen at the hospital yesterday?"

"Nothing happened. I had a good time with one of the patients. I'm concerned about him."

"The Jacoby boy—your father's told me about him."

Meg sat upright. "Has Dad said how Donovan's doing today?"

"I'm trying to get him off for a little relaxation. I asked him not to even call in today. If he's needed, he'll be paged."

Meg had seen her mother's efforts to protect

her father from overwork before. She planned frequent getaways and weekend minitrips. Still, most jaunts were interrupted by calls from the hospital, moreso now that he was head of the transplant unit. "Go on to the golf course," Meg said. "I'm perfectly fine by myself."

Once they were gone, Meg tried to lounge by the pool and read a book, but she couldn't concentrate on the story. Her thoughts kept returning to Donovan, his medical prognosis, JWC, and the One Last Wish Foundation. Around five o'clock, she gave up, dressed, and left her parents a note: "Went for a drive to buy some frozen yogurt. Don't worry, Mom. I'll get the low-fat. Honest."

She hoped the note's levity would keep them from being concerned about her. She was in the pits emotionally and was attempting to take her therapist's advice—"stay busy, stay involved."

Meg wasn't sure how she ended up near the hospital, but before she knew it, she was pulling her car off the exit ramp that would take her to Memorial. The neighborhood around the complex was well kept. Older houses, once the homes of Washington's elite, dominated the area to the north, away from the expressway. To the west side of the hospital, signs announced the construction of sleek new medical office buildings. Meg saw the whole area as an odd mixture of the old and the new, with a sturdy median strip lined with cherry trees separating the past from the present.

As she neared the entrance of Memorial, Meg recognized Mrs. Jacoby and Brett waiting at the bus stop. She pulled to a halt in front of them. "How are you?" she asked.

Brett waved. "Hi," he said. "I remember you."

Mrs. Jacoby's face looked lined and drawn, and Meg's heart went out to her. "Come on," Meg urged, throwing open her car door. "Let me give you a ride home."

"We live too far," Mrs. Jacoby said.

"No problem. I'd love to take you."

"Are you sure?"

"Positive," Meg replied, knowing instantly it was the truth. She wanted to know Donovan's family better, and she wanted to help. She couldn't change the past, but she could affect the future. "Hop in and tell me all about Donovan. I have a ton of questions for you."

# Eight

❧

Brett bounded into the backseat, and Donovan's mother wearily got into the front. "This is very nice of you. For some reason, the bus doesn't seem to run on schedule on Sundays."

"Hey, this car is neat!" Brett blurted, bouncing on the leather seat. "Is it yours?"

"It's mine," Meg said.

"Put on your seat belt," his mother insisted.

"That's the rule in my car," Meg told him as he began to protest. When she heard the buckle snap into place, she asked, "So, how was Donovan today?"

"Crabby," Brett announced.

"He wasn't feeling well," Mrs. Jacoby explained. "Dr. Rosenthal said his electrolytes were imbalanced and his potassium levels were elevated. It's happened before, and it always makes Donovan spacey and incoherent. The doctor says it's hard on his heart too."

"He kept talking like we were back home," Brett chimed in. "He kept telling me to call Lauren for him and tell her he was picking her up for their date. That's dumb."

"I explained it was because his blood was messed up," Mrs. Jacoby said over her shoulder. "He didn't know what he was saying."

"He didn't even listen when I told him about the fort I'm making in my bedroom."

"Please, Brett, he couldn't help it."

Meg thought Mrs. Jacoby sounded on the verge of tears. "I have an idea," Meg said. "Before I take you home, how'd you like some ice cream? My treat."

"Yeah!" Brett's voice filled the car. "Chocolate."

"Don't go out of your way for us."

"I was going to get some for myself when I saw you. There's a minimall not too far from here."

"It's kind of you," Mrs. Jacoby said. "I don't want any, but Brett will follow you anywhere if you feed him."

Meg laughed. When she reached a small strip center, she parked and the three of them went inside an ice-cream parlor decorated like an old-time country store. They ordered, and while they waited, Mrs. Jacoby handed Brett two quarters for a game machine tucked back in a corner. While he was preoccupied, Mrs. Jacoby leaned against the booth and shut her eyes. "I'm exhausted. Thanks again for offering us a ride."

"Too bad you live so far away from the hospital."

"Believe me, I tried to get closer, but the immediate vicinity had no rental apartments. I'm afraid the homes there are out of my league."

"Donovan told me about your home in Virginia. He misses it."

"So do I, but once we were told he had to have a liver transplant, I knew we had to be closer to the transplant center. The call could come anytime, day or night. The closer we are, the sooner we can get here. I'm sure you understand how critical timing is for something like this."

Meg nodded. "Maybe the call will come soon."

"Maybe. I have mixed feelings, however."

"You do?"

"Think about it. His life, the liver he so desperately needs, depends on someone else's dying. I think about that. I think about some mother losing her child, and it makes my heart ache. But my son is living on borrowed time—every day is one less that he has to live. And every day brings him closer to either dying or surviving with a part of another mother's child inside his body. These days, medical science gives us strange choices."

"Sometimes it seems like doctors play God, doesn't it?" Meg asked.

"Don't get me wrong . . . I'm grateful for the technology, grateful for men like your father who've devoted their lives to bringing recovery and longevity to the dying. Organ transplantation is a wonderful thing, but human beings are always involved, and that makes it complex, not simple at all. Life and death never is." Mrs. Jacoby studied Meg and smiled sheepishly. "I'm sorry. I didn't mean to get so philosophical. It's been a long day."

"Now that you've moved to the city, will you stay even after Donovan's transplant?"

"I assume so. He'll need to be checked regularly, and of course, his dosage of immune-suppressant drugs will have to be carefully regulated. Washington's not such a bad place to raise two sons. There's plenty of history here. And the suburbs really are lovely, although I'm positive I couldn't afford anything too grand. Still, there must be some nice neighborhoods I'll be able to afford someday." She laughed wryly and added, "Tonight, I'd trade a mansion in the boondocks for a room with a view nearer the hospital. This commute is the pits."

Once again, Meg realized how sheltered her own life had been. She'd lived in the same house since she was a baby, and she took her life-style for granted. "If you had a car—" she started.

"I couldn't afford the insurance. No, for now, this is simply the way things have to be. I'm resigned to it."

The ice cream arrived, and Brett bolted over to the table and dug in. Meg enjoyed his enthusiasm, and soon the three of them were laughing over his stories about taking his laser gun to school. Yet, subconsciously, Meg kept mulling over Mrs. Jacoby's dilemma. How terrible it would be to have someone in the hospital and no way to get to him quickly. She wondered if Donovan would want to spend a portion of his Wish money on transportation for his mom. She decided that as soon as he was feeling better, she would ask him.

When Meg arrived for work Monday morning, she went by the nurses' station in order to get an update on Donovan's medical status. "His blood work hasn't come up from the lab yet," Mrs. Vasquez said. "But he seems more coherent this morning."

"My brother would get the same way when his blood chemistry got out of whack. Once Donovan's balanced, he'll be back in his right mind," Alana told Meg.

Meg tried to feel encouraged, but she didn't want to see Donovan not in control of his facilities. Something cautioned her that he wouldn't want her to see him that way either. Around lunchtime, she overcame her inhibitions and went to his room anyway. He lay on his side, staring into space.

"Hello," she said cautiously. His eyes slowly focused on her face. He attempted to sit up, but she put her hand on his shoulder to keep him down. "I can't stay but a minute."

He nodded and held his arm slightly aloft. An IV line led to a pole beside his bed where clear plastic bags hung. "As you can tell, my friend and I are reattached." Donovan's voice sounded hoarse.

"That's what friends are for."

"I hate this one," he whispered. "He cramps my style."

"I'm sure you won't need him in a couple of days." She told him about taking his mom and Brett for ice cream and then home to their apartment.

"What did you think of our castle?"

She couldn't tell him that she found the place small and depressing. "It was interesting. Your Mom's fixed it up pretty nice." His gaze never left her face, and soon she felt her cheeks burning. "You should call Brett later. He thought you were being mean to him yesterday because you were so out of it. He can't quite catch on to what's happening."

"Me either," Donovan said glumly.

"Brett said you kept asking for Lauren. Do you miss her?" Meg wasn't sure why she was asking. It wasn't any of her business, but she wanted to know, needed to know.

"No. I miss what she represents—freedom from this place. The life I used to have before I got sick."

"After your transplant, you'll be able to have your old life back."

"How can a person go back after he's been through something like this? How can I ever feel normal again?"

She wanted to tell him she understood perfectly what he was saying. She wanted to tell him about what she had been through during the past year. Instead, she asked, "What's normal anyhow, and who decides? Let's make our own 'normal.'"

"I need a favor," he said after a moment.

"Name it."

"I need you to find out if the money from the Wish Foundation is really mine to spend on whatever I want. When I got sick, I started thinking I could die and never spend the money, and that wouldn't be right. My family needs the money."

"I'll see what I can find out," Meg assured him, even though she hadn't a clue as to how to go about it.

"You have to figure out a way of getting the information without telling anyone I received it."

"I'll take care of it." She hoped with every fiber of her being that the money would be his completely. Donovan deserved it. JWC must think so too, or why else would Donovan have been chosen?

Meg returned to work, determined to find out what she could. She hung around the hospital after her shift ended, until she knew that her father was alone in his office. Meg hurried to corner him before some medical emergency called him away.

"Are you busy?" she asked, stepping into his office and closing the door.

"Not at the moment. Come on in."

He was all smiles, obviously in a good mood,

and she didn't want to ruin it. "You look happy," she said.

"My heart transplant patient is doing so splendidly that I'm going to release her at the end of the week. I love it when things go off without a hitch."

"That's super." Meg felt her heart hammering against her ribs as she struggled with a way to phrase her questions on Donovan's behalf. "I was wondering if you could tell me something."

"I'll try."

Meg took a deep breath. "Can someone who's been accepted for your transplant program be kicked out of it?"

# Nine

"Kicked out?" Meg's father sounded puzzled. "It's not a social club, Meg. We don't admit people into the program lightly. We conduct medical as well as psychological tests—interviews with psychiatrists and other doctors to determine if a person can handle undergoing a transplant. Not everyone is a candidate, but once a patient is admitted, he stays until either we find a matching donor or he dies waiting for one."

"And so if the money part's already handled, it won't matter if someone waiting to get a transplant gets rich all of a sudden? What I mean is, what if someone needs a transplant and he's accepted and the cost is already covered and then that person wins the lottery or something. Will he have to pay for his own transplant just because he's gotten filthy rich?"

"Once funds have been allocated for a patient, his medical procedures are covered, no matter how rich he gets. But there are many costs following the transplant that the patient will incur," her father replied.

"Such as?"

"A changed life-style. The immune-suppressant drugs. They can run upward of ten thousand dollars annually."

"That's a lot of money." Meg's elation over Donovan's being able to keep his Wish money quickly vanished.

"But those drugs allow a patient years more of life. How can you put a price on that?" He steepled his fingers together and eyed her quizzically. "Why all this interest in finances?"

Meg thought quickly, then replied, "I've been noticing things this hospital could use."

"Such as?"

"For instance, why isn't there a hotel nearby for a patient's family to stay at while they wait around for a transplant?"

"I admit it would be very helpful, but land around here is at a premium. This area was all residential until Memorial was built, but slowly, over the years, people have moved to the suburbs. Ever since the transplant program's come in, Memorial's grown even more."

"It bothers me that people like Mrs. Jacoby have to live so far away. I'll bet Donovan would like to have her closer. And it must really be hard on littler kids. I see their parents sleeping in their rooms in chairs, or even on the couches in the waiting rooms. They don't look very comfortable."

"You're right. I wish we had a special house for patients' families. A big corporation talked about building one years ago, but then they thought the need was greater for one near the children's cancer facility in Maryland, so they built one up there. Without their financial backing, our project never got off the ground."

"But Memorial still needs one—especially now, for people waiting for transplants."

"It would take a couple of years to get such a project going."

"Why?"

"I remember when we looked into it before. All monies had to be raised from scratch. An architect was needed to draw up plans, building materials had to be bought or donated, furnishings acquired, not to mention kitchen and bathroom fixtures, recreational areas for leisure time, people to manage the facility, volunteers to help out—I'm telling you, Meg, it's a mammoth undertaking."

"But it seems to me as if you need it now more than ever." She tried not to be dismayed over the length of his list.

"I agree, but even if we had the land and the money, the actual building of this kind of facility could take close to a year of construction work."

"You have to start sometime." Meg wasn't sure why she felt so strongly in favor of the idea. She'd never been a crusader. Maybe it was seeing how Donovan's mother was struggling to keep her family together. Or having to comfort some of the kids on the pediatric floor when they were sobbing because they missed their mothers. Or maybe it was knowing what Cindy's family had gone through. All the things together caused her to imagine such a house vividly. "I can't believe this hospital can't spare some of its land to build a home away from home for patients' families."

Her father eyed her thoughtfully. "The land's only one hurdle. What about the rest of it? Money doesn't grow on trees."

"What if some group took it on as a project?"

"That would be nice. Any ideas?"

"A couple."

"Then go for it."

"What?" His answer drew her up short. "*Me* do something?"

"You're the one with the ideas. And I know how determined you can get once you set your mind on something." She opened her mouth to argue, but he continued, saying, "Aren't you the girl who staged a sit-down strike in the school cafeteria in the eighth grade to protest the quality of the food?"

Of course she remembered the event, but Cindy had been her cohort, and together they had masterminded the demonstration.

"And *won*?" her father added.

"That was different. This is serious."

"I know it's serious. I'm not telling you to raise the money yourself, only to find a group to spearhead such a project. I have faith in you. I think you can do it."

Meg wanted to argue against the idea. She wanted to tell her father that all she'd agreed to do this summer was be a volunteer. But even as she silently listed her reasons for not tackling such a project, she knew it intrigued her. And all because of someone whose initials were JWC. If this anonymous person could calmly drop one hundred thousand dollars into Donovan Jacoby's lap, then why couldn't Meg do something of equal or even greater value for him?

All the way home, Meg warred with herself about such an undertaking. A part of her said, "You're sixteen. You can't do this." But another part of her argued, "Why not? All you have to do is discuss it with Mom and ask how one of her Junior League projects gets going. Maybe the League could be the spearhead group that Dad mentioned. The worst that can happen is the idea won't work."

That evening, she broached the idea with her mother. "We have many worthwhile projects," her mother told Meg after she'd listened carefully.

"Don't you think this one is worthwhile?"

"Yes, I do. However, I'm only one board member. There are others who'll need convincing."

"Can't you convince them?"

Her mother put her hand on Meg's shoulder. "I

could never do it as well as you. Perhaps you can speak to them at our next board meeting."

Meg groaned. What had she gotten herself into?

A week later, Meg found herself standing in front of the Junior League's board of directors in her own living room, her heart hammering as she made her case.

"I have a friend at Memorial who's dying. He needs a transplant, and he needs his family near him while he waits for one. You probably can't help him with his transplant, but you can help his family get closer than an hour's ride away from him."

Meg had prepared for the presentation. She had statistics and logical arguments. She made a strong case for an immediate and concentrated fund-raising effort. Appealing to the emotions of those women in the room, she spoke of a mother's love for her child, a family's need to be involved with their loved one's care, a patient's longing to have someone he loves near him to ease emotional and physical suffering.

When Meg wrapped up her talk, she knew by the women's expressions that she had had an impact. She silently hoped it had been strong enough to persuade the board to take up the project of building a special guest house.

"Thank you, Meg," Mrs. Hotchkiss, the president, said. "We'll discuss your suggestion and get back to you."

Meg was disappointed. She had hoped they'd

say yes on the spot. The next day over lunch, she confided in Alana, who'd become a pal.

"I think it's a dynamite idea," Alana said. "My brother will too. In fact, I'll bet if we get endorsements from all the people who've gotten transplants at this place, we could make one *fine* fund-raising letter."

"I'll bet you're right," Meg agreed, warming to the suggestion. "Maybe we could ask local reporters to feature stories about former patients. Would Lonnie volunteer for an interview?"

"Of course. Especially if his sister strong-arms him." Alana giggled. "Lonnie's working for a big company in Washington. Maybe they will cough up some big bucks. Maybe we can talk folks into being Santa in July."

"Why not? For every gift Santa leaves, he could take up a donation for our cause."

"We'll be Santa's special elves."

Meg laughed. The home away from home for the families of sick people was no laughing matter, but somehow the joking made the task seem less insurmountable. Laughing with Alana about grandiose plans such as building a place was just plain fun.

Fun. Wasn't that what had been missing in her life for over a year? What an odd place to get it, Meg thought. Through the lives of people she hadn't even known six weeks before.

# Ten

By THE END of the week, Meg had no news about her project, but good news about Donovan. His blood chemistry had stabilized, his IV had been removed, and he was in good spirits. "It's a six-hour pass for Saturday from your father," he said, waving a piece of paper under Meg's nose. "Where do you want to take me?"

"Where do you want to go?"

"Besides Alaska? I'd like to go home." His expression grew wistful, then he said, "Mom wants us over for dinner at the apartment. Would you come with me?"

"I'd love to," Meg said, realizing she was his sole means of transportation and that without her, it would cost him a fortune in cab fare to get to his mother's apartment. "I'll bet your Mom's a good cook."

"Even the dying get a final meal."

"Don't joke about that."

Donovan took her hand. "Sorry. Being cooped up for so long has blackened my sense of humor. Promise me something."

"What?"

"Before we go to my mom's, let's have some fun on our own."

She smiled. "You're on."

Donovan checked out of the hospital on Saturday afternoon, and Meg started their outing with a drive down Pennsylvania Avenue, past the White House. "Think we should stop in and say hello to the Prez?" Donovan asked. "I think he should allocate more funding for transplants. There's not enough money for people who need them."

"He's out of the city—too hot this time of the year."

"Great. Where's government in action when I need it?"

"Have you seen the Washington Monument? How about the Lincoln Memorial?" She tried to think of things that didn't require much walking, since Donovan was still recovering.

"I've never seen them," he admitted. "The most I've seen is the inside of Memorial Hospital."

Meg took him to the Washington Monument first. The great obelisk soared upward from the green grass into the bright blue sky. People had spread blankets on the grass, and children ran squealing and trailing kites. Meg thought the air humid and muggy, but Donovan insisted the warmth felt good. "I've been cooped up so long in the hospital, I feel like a mushroom," he told her.

They walked toward the Lincoln Memorial, along the rectangular Reflecting Pool, then sat beside the cool water, where Meg watched reflections of clouds float on the water's surface. She hoped Donovan wasn't overly exerting himself.

"Do you know how tired I am of being sick?" Donovan asked with a sigh. "Sometimes I don't think they'll ever find a donor for me."

"Sure they will." Meg tried to sound confident. "You've come this far."

"Far?" He gave a sarcastic chuckle. "Far from what? My home? My friends? Look what my mother's had to sacrifice for me. I think about all she's had to give up because I'm sick."

"Don't think about it. Think about all the things you'll get to do once your transplant is over."

"Like what?"

"Like spend your Wish money. You could buy your mom a car." Meg had already told him how she had talked to her father and confirmed that Donovan's medical expenses would be covered regardless of his personal finances. The One Last Wish check was his to keep and spend as he wanted.

"No . . . I want to get her something really awesome. She could use a new house." Donovan sat up straighter the moment the words were out of his mouth. He turned and looked at Meg with an expression of total revelation. "That's it. That's what I can buy her. I haven't told her anything yet."

"A house is a big deal, all right. Don't you think your mother might like to pick out her own?"

"But then it won't be a surprise. That's the part that would make it special. She'd be surprised— the way I was surprised when I discovered the Wish money and decided it was for real. I can't tell you how it felt to open that letter and see that check. And then to know it was mine—all mine—to do anything I wanted with. Well, what I *want* is to buy my mother a house."

"Houses cost lots of money."

"I have a ton of money."

"But it still may not be enough."

"I won't know until I start looking." Donovan took her by her shoulders. "You can help me."

Meg blinked. "How? I don't know the first thing about looking for a house."

"How hard can it be? When we sold ours in Virginia, Mom hired a real estate agent. She showed the house to a bunch of people, and one of them bought it. That seems simple enough to me."

"I know how the process works," Meg said. "I just don't know what I can do to help."

"You can help me find an agent. You can tell her how much money I have to work with. And about how I need to be near the hospital. It needs to be a nice neighborhood, one with good schools for Brett."

Meg noticed that Donovan had excluded himself from the school agenda. "Gee, I don't know . . ."

"Meg, please, I need you. I need you to be my arms and legs while I'm stuck at Memorial."

She looked into his eyes and saw quiet desperation. *He needed her.* His appeal sliced deep into her heart. She needed him too. Needed him in her life, even though she couldn't explain why to either one of them. "Well, I guess I could ask around for you."

"I knew I could count on you."

She wanted to tell him not to get his hopes up. "I'm not even positive I can persuade a real estate agent to talk to me. I mean, I don't look old enough to have the kind of money it takes for a house. An agent will think I'm a fraud."

"So tell her you're a rock star." He grinned. "Everybody knows rock stars are young, rich, and weird."

"A rock star! Who would believe that?"

"You'll think of something. I have complete confidence in you."

Meg didn't feel confident at all, but she knew she would try her best for his sake. "Listen, Mr. Moneybags, if I somehow manage to bamboozle some agent and get her to take me, *you*, on as a client, and I line up some houses for you to see, then you have to do your part, understand?"

"What's that?"

"You have to stay well."

He cupped her chin in his palm. "I'm doing my best. With my luck, I'll find the perfect house and just before I close the deal, my beeper will go off and your father will want to give me a transplant."

Meg gazed deeply into his eyes. "May you have such good luck," she said. "May you have such good luck."

The meal Donovan's mother prepared for them that evening was simple, but tasty. "It's terrific, Mom," he told her.

Meg agreed, looking around the apartment at Mrs. Jacoby's meager belongings and well-worn furniture. Through the walls, Meg could hear a baby crying and a television blaring in neighboring apartments.

Brett bounced enthusiastically in his chair. "We can spend the night together," he said. His face fell when Donovan told him that he had to return to the hospital. "But that's not fair. Why can't you stay?"

"Because I'm still sick. I don't want to go back, but I have to."

"You've been gone a long time. I want you to come home."

"I can't, Brett."

Brett pushed away from the table. "You could if you wanted. Me and Mom can take care of you."

"I have to leave."

"I hate you!" Brett shouted, his eyes filling with

tears. "I don't want you to come home. Stay at your stupid hospital forever."

"Brett—" Mrs. Jacoby called as he ran down the hall and slammed into his bedroom. "I'll go get him."

Donovan stood. "No. Let me talk to him. It's me he's mad at."

"He doesn't mean it, you know."

"I know." Donovan disappeared down the hall.

Meg understood perfectly how Brett felt. Hadn't she been angry—*furious*—about Cindy? In her pain, hadn't she wanted to strike out at everybody? "He'll get over it," Meg said in the awkward silence that remained in the room. "He'll feel sorry for being mean to Donovan and will want to see him as soon as possible, just to make sure his anger didn't harm Donovan in some way."

Mrs. Jacoby looked at Meg. "You're right. It's happened before. He cries and worries that his brother will get sicker. How did you know?"

Meg averted her eyes. "I'm a doctor's daughter, remember? I could call him later, after I check Donovan back in to the hospital, and let him know that all's well."

"You'd do that?"

"Sure. Brett feels left out, and that makes him feel worse because he knows Donovan's really sick and he can't make it go away."

"You're a smart and tenderhearted girl, Meg. I appreciate all you're doing. For both my sons."

Meg shrugged. She liked Mrs. Jacoby and Brett. And she liked Donovan too. Liked him more than she knew she should, given his circumstances. *He's going to beat the odds*, she told herself. The Network for Organ Sharing would find him a liver, and he'd have the transplant, recover, and be all right. He had to be.

Meg checked Donovan back in to the hospital that evening. "Don't forget to help find my mother a house," he said as he crawled into bed.

He looked awfully exhausted to Meg. "I won't," she promised. She drove home and went to bed, but couldn't fall asleep. She was still tossing when she heard the phone ring at two A.M. She realized it would be for her father, and felt a vague sense of foreboding she couldn't explain. When she heard his footsteps in the hall, she got out of bed and met him at the top of the stairs.

"I'm sorry if the phone woke you," he said, startled by her appearance. "Go back to bed."

Something in the way he averted his eyes made her ask, "What's wrong? Is there something wrong with someone I know? With Donovan?"

Her father looked at her fully, hesitated, then said, "That was a call from a hospital in Bethesda, Maryland. I'm driving over there now because they have an accident victim on the verge of brain death, and his blood type is the same as Donovan's."

# Eleven

⁓

"ARE YOU SAYING they've found a donor for Donovan?" Meg's heart began to race in anticipation.

"Don't jump to that conclusion. All I know is that the victim meets several criteria that *could* make him a match. I'm going over there to be available for organ retrieval, just in case."

"I want to come with you." The words jumped from Meg's throat.

"Meg, that's not necessary. The family hasn't even been approached about donating yet, and there would be nothing for you to do but hang around the waiting room."

She caught his arm. "Please, Dad, let me come along. I-I've never asked for anything like this before. Don't say no. It's really important to me."

Her father studied her intently, as if weighing

his medical professionalism and his role as her father. "I need to leave now."

"Five minutes," she pleaded. "I can be dressed to go in five minutes." Her heart hammered as she waited for his reply.

"All right," he said, jangling the keys in his pocket. "I'll leave your mother a note. Meet me in the garage."

Meg spun, ran to her room, tugged on clothes, grabbed her purse, and raced down the stairs. They rode in silence along the Beltway through sparse traffic, toward the Maryland exit. She watched her father pick up his car phone and call Memorial. "I want you to prep Donovan Jacoby for surgery," she heard him tell an assistant on his transplant team. "Start him on the donor protocol, and I'll let you know as soon as possible if I'm able to retrieve."

"Will Donovan know he may get the transplant tonight?" she asked when her father hung up the receiver.

"He'll know. We'll do blood work, an EKG, and X rays. Then we'll start him on antibiotics and antirejection drugs right away."

"What if he doesn't get the organ?"

"We have to prepare as if he will. We have to lower his risk for postoperative infection and give him a head start on organ acceptance. As for the other—well, the specter of disappointment, of not getting the new organ, is something all potential transplant recipients have to learn to live with."

Meg watched the lampposts flash past the car window as her father sped along the expressway. She felt events were hurtling by just as fast. She pictured Donovan's face as he heard that he might get his new liver. She knew how he longed for the waiting to be over. "I hope this is it for him."

"I hope so too."

At the Bethesda hospital, Meg followed her father up stairwells and through a maze of long corridors. He paused in front of a set of double doors marked "Personnel Only Beyond This Point." He glanced about. "There'll be a waiting room nearby. Go there and wait for me while I check with the trauma team. The patient's on life support, but I want to make sure he's being well oxygenated."

Meg found her way to a cubbyhole of a room, where six people were gathered together in a small huddle. Their grief hit her like a wall the moment she walked inside the room. She wanted to back out slowly, but realized they had taken no notice of her, so she slunk to a chair. Her palms felt clammy and her mouth dry. She fumbled in her purse for a mint.

"We can't lose him," Meg heard a woman sob.

"They're doing all they can, Peggy. We just have to wait," the man beside her said.

Meg sucked in her breath. This had to be the potential donor's family. Meg lowered her gaze, trying to make herself as small and as inconspicuous as possible, wishing she'd chosen any room but this one to wait for her father.

"He's still alive," another woman said. "The police said he was alive when the ambulance left the accident."

Meg experienced a wave of horror. The person they were talking about wasn't alive. She'd heard her father mention brain death on his car phone. She felt guilty withholding the information, but knew there was nothing she could do or say.

"Remember when Blake was little?" the woman asked. "Remember how he'd drive his trike to the end of the driveway for hours on end? Then, when he got his driver's license, he was happy. So full of life."

"Don't do this to yourself, Mama," a young woman said.

"Do I remember? How could I not remember? He was my baby." She broke into quiet sobs, and the man beside her put his arms around her.

Meg felt desperately sorry for them. Death meant going away forever. It meant leaving families and friends behind. It meant leaving a hole in time and space that only that one special person could fill up. She understood that part— understood it very well. She began to grow queasy.

Two men and a woman entered the waiting room. Meg could tell at a glance that they were medical personnel. "Dr. Burnside!" the woman cried. "How's Blake? How's my son?"

The doctor took her hands and pulled her to

her feet. "Peggy, I want you and your family to come into the conference room with me. I want my colleagues to talk to all of you." He nodded toward the other man and the woman.

"Are they surgeons? Does my Blake need some special kind of operation? Whatever he needs, doctor, do it."

"Come, let's go where there's more privacy." Dr. Burnside's gaze flicked over Meg.

Her cheeks burned, and she stared stonily into space. Once they all left the room, Meg released her breath, startled that she'd been holding it all this time. The room seemed too quiet, and she wished her father would come. Maybe she should have stayed home after all. She had no idea how long the operation to remove the boy's—she couldn't bring herself to say his name—organs would take. Not long, she figured. She knew how critical a factor time was in transplantation. *Just a little bit longer, Donovan,* she told herself. His wait was practically over.

Meg lost track of time, but when her father appeared at the doorway, she was surprised. Somehow, it didn't seem long enough for him to have completed his tasks. There was no liveliness about him either, no undercurrent of raw energy, as she often saw when he was facing a transplant surgery. "Are you finished?" she asked haltingly.

He came over and sat heavily in the chair beside her. For the first time, she noticed lines of fatigue around his eyes and mouth. "There isn't going to be any surgery," he said.

"There isn't? Why not?"

"The family refused to grant permission."

His words hit her like stones. "B-but they have to. Don't they know Donovan's dying?"

Her father took her hand. "Honey, they don't know Donovan. All they know is their eighteen-year-old son is dead."

"Didn't you try to change their minds? Didn't you tell them how important it was?"

"Organ donation is voluntary, Meg. People can't be forced."

She felt panic well up inside her. "So, what will they do with him? Just shove him into the ground? Just let his organs go to waste when they could be put into someone else and help him live longer?"

"You can't think about it that way. You have to understand and respect their feelings."

"Well, I don't!" Meg tore her hand from her father's and stood. Her legs felt rubbery, but she began to pace. "It's not fair. Why wouldn't they? Why wouldn't they say yes?"

"People have a hundred reasons." He shook his head. "They're afraid of disfiguring their loved one—which we don't. They feel it's freakish to transfer body parts from one person to another. Too many Frankenstein movies," he added. "Whatever their reasons, we can't intervene. We can't ever force anyone to agree to donation. It's a tough thing to even broach with grieving relatives. I told you that once before."

She remembered, recalling her own feelings

about transplantation. Hadn't she herself once been turned off to the whole idea? Yet, now that she knew Donovan, her feelings had completely changed. "So, why do you even bother to ask at all? Why get somebody's hopes up for nothing?"

"First of all, we ask because it's the law. We *have* to ask. Second, because there are many people who realize that this is the ultimate gift to others and an opportunity to do something good and kind. This is a way for their loved one to continue living."

"But not these people," Meg said. "These people don't care about others at all."

Her father came quickly alongside her. He took her arms and turned her to face him. "Don't ever say that, Meg. These people just had their son die, and they are inconsolable."

Meg began to tremble, understanding exactly what inconsolable felt like. It was a deep, black hole. A bottomless well of tears and anguish. A place without sunlight or even air. Her lip began to quiver. "I don't want Donovan to die, Daddy."

Her father drew her into his arms. "I'm doing all I can, Meg. There'll be another donor for him. You have to believe that."

She nodded, forcing down the tears that were trying to burst free. "I thought this was it for him. I thought his waiting was over."

He looked down into her face with troubled eyes. "Meg, medicine is a strange business. It's life and death. Sometimes it's making choices that no one but God should have to make. I know what you're feeling because I've felt that way myself. I want to tell you something, and I want you to listen closely."

"I'm listening."

"The only way to treat patients and not go crazy is to distance yourself from them. You can't allow yourself to become so personally involved that you lose your professional perspective. Do you understand what I'm telling you?"

"Yes. You think I'm overreacting."

"No, your concern is all too human. But you can't become too personally involved in any one case or in any one patient's life. It's the first rule of the doctor-patient relationship."

She took a deep breath, forcing down a retort. She wasn't a doctor. Nor did she ever want to be. Medicine was her father's world, and she was sorry she'd gotten mixed up in it at all. "Don't you ever get involved, Dad? Doesn't someone ever become special to you?"

He shrugged and glanced away. "It's a fine line to walk. I have to watch myself. My patients are just that—patients. No matter how hard I try, I can't save them all."

She tried to apply brakes to her runaway emotions. She took a deep breath and attempted to distance herself from the drama she had just witnessed. "I'm all right now," she said. "I-I'm sorry I got so angry."

"It's understandable." He ran his hand through his hair. "Now, I've got the tough job of telling Donovan."

"Will you tell him now?"

"I'll take you home first, then go check on him. My transplant team knows there won't be any surgery. Donovan will be fairly groggy for the next couple of days, but sooner or later, he'll figure out he didn't have the transplant. You're right about one thing—he's going to be a very disappointed young man."

Her heart squeezed as renewed concern for Donovan swept through her. She was going to have to face his disappointment also. Meg took a deep breath and followed her father out into the hall. If professional distance was one of her father's rules, she knew she was in trouble. She'd already broken it and could figure no way to turn the situation around.

# Twelve

"You're dragging around today, Meg. Did you have a hot date last night?" Alana asked.

Meg shook her head in response and sipped a soda, hoping the cola would revive her sagging energies. The lunch crowd in the hospital cafeteria seemed especially loud to her. "I wish it had been a hot date. No, I'm afraid last night was a real downer for me." Quickly, she recounted her and her father's false alarm run to Bethesda for Donovan. "I didn't get to bed until four A.M. and then I couldn't go to sleep. I feel like a zombie today. Sorry if I'm not carrying my share of the work on the floor."

"Forget it. I'm just sorry the donor didn't work out for Donovan. Have you been by to see him this morning?"

"Not yet. Frankly, I'm not looking forward to talking to him. I know how depressed he's going to be, and I feel so helpless. I don't know what to say to him. I mean, how do you go about consoling someone because he didn't get a transplant? Someone who's still living on borrowed time?"

Alana's expression was sympathetic. "You know I understand because of my brother's situation. I wish I could help people understand that."

"I wish I could help the whole *world* understand it," Meg countered. "The truth is, unless it happens to someone you care about, it isn't important to you."

Alana started stacking the empty plates from Meg's lunch tray onto her own. "You've got some free time. Why don't you go see Donovan now?"

"He's still in ICU and won't be brought back to his room until tomorrow. Maybe by tomorrow, I'll feel better myself. I don't want to make him even more depressed."

"He doesn't have to know about your going to the other hospital with your father. And all you have to do is hold his hand and listen to him. Don't feel you have to be responsible for making him cheerful. Sometimes, it's okay to let a person work through his anger by himself."

Meg thought Alana sounded very wise. "The voice of experience?" she asked.

Alana nodded. "Sometimes all I could do for my brother was listen. He needed to get it out, and I was the one person in our family who let him say anything he felt like saying." She smiled impishly. "And sometimes that boy had some pretty shocking things to say. I didn't know he knew such words."

Meg felt a flood of gratitude toward her friend. Maybe it would be best not to tell Donovan how upset she'd gotten over the family's refusal to donate their dead son's organs. "I'll remember what you said." She touched Alana's arm. "And thanks for the advice."

Alana smiled. "Anytime."

Two days later, Meg could visit with Donovan. Even after he was brought down from ICU, he was still incoherent. Meg spent time with Mrs. Jacoby during one of her visits to the hospital. They met in one of the pediatric playrooms, where Brett, well out of earshot, was building a spaceship with giant snap-together blocks.

"The night the hospital called me, I almost went delirious with joy," Donovan's mother told Meg, sighing. "I thought it was finally happening for him. I bundled up Brett and took a cab to the hospital. The two of us waited and waited. Brett fell asleep—thank heaven—but I couldn't think about anything except Donovan's surgery."

"And then there was no surgery," Meg commented. "You must have really felt cheated when you found out."

"I felt both disappointed and relieved at the same time."

"I don't understand."

"Disappointed for the obvious reasons. Relieved because the unknowns are so scary for me.

I mean, once he has the transplant, he has a long road of recovery ahead. Also, once it's done, there's no turning back. If his new liver rejects, or if something goes wrong, Donovan will certainly die. I know I shouldn't borrow trouble, but that fear always lurks in the back of my mind."

Meg swallowed her own taste of fear. "I guess you're right. Even though he's sick, even though his own liver's failing, at least he's alive."

Mrs. Jacoby patted Meg's hand. "I shouldn't dump my doubts and fears on you. Forgive me. There are people here at the hospital—psychologists—I should be talking to."

"I don't mind," Meg said quickly.

"No, it's not fair to you. My only excuse is that you're so genuinely concerned about my son."

"I am, Mrs. Jacoby. I care about him so much." Meg felt her cheeks redden after her impassioned words. Donovan's mother must think she sounded like a moonstruck child.

Mrs. Jacoby smiled with understanding. "He had a girlfriend back home. I wish she'd been half as caring and sensitive as you. I'm afraid she really hurt him."

"It was *her* loss," Meg said, realizing she wasn't Donovan's girlfriend in the sense Mrs. Jacoby meant. Still, she truly cared about him.

"I agree. Have you heard anything more about building that special house where parents can stay and be near their kids while they're being treated here at Memorial?" Donovan's mother changed the subject. "Believe me, I sure wished for one the other night. I think that cab ride back to the apartment after I learned there would be no transplant was the longest ride I've ever taken. All I wanted to do was tuck Brett in and curl up and go to sleep myself, but I couldn't. We had to traipse all the way back across town first."

Meg shook her head. "Sorry . . . I haven't heard anything yet."

"Oh, well . . . It is a big undertaking." She made a face. "Poor choice of words."

*Undertaking.* Meg caught the meaning. Undertaker. She shivered, even though the playroom was sunny and warm.

The next day, when Meg went to Donovan's room, he was sitting up in bed, flipping through TV channels. Seeing him upright and alert caused a rush of relief. "You must be better," she said, coming inside. "You're scanning the TV wasteland."

He flipped off the screen and held out his hand to her. "I'm better," he said. "Whatever that means."

She took his hand, noticing that his color looked strange—somewhere between yellow and pasty white. But his voice sounded strong and lucid once more. "It means that you'll be hanging around until another potential liver donor comes along," she said.

"I was pretty out of it, wasn't I?"

"Do you remember anything?"

"I remember being awakened in the middle of

the night by some nurse promising me a wild and crazy time."

Meg giggled. "She didn't lie, did she?"

"They put me on a gurney and wheeled me down to the operating room. They did a bunch of tests and forced a Krom's cocktail down me."

"What's that?"

"The most foul-tasting stuff ever invented by medical science. It's a decontaminant for your intestinal area, you know—to kill off all the nasty germs lurking inside the body. That way, once you have the transplant, your body has a better chance of accepting the new organ."

"Too bad it was for nothing," Meg said.

"Yeah . . . too bad. But, then, I never did have much good luck."

She braced herself against a wave of pity for him. She'd learned that patients don't want pity, they want understanding. "You've had some good luck. You met me," she quipped.

A smile softened Donovan's face, and in spite of his gauntness, she felt her pulse quicken. "Okay, so I'll give you that one."

"What else did they do to you?"

"They gave me a preop shot that sent me off to never-never land, so I was kind of spaced out. I remember my mom coming in to see me. Then I don't remember anything else for the next twenty-four hours. I just woke up in ICU. It took me a while to figure out that something had gone wrong with the transplant, because I knew I'd have big staples in my side from the operation and I didn't." He shook his head, as if clearing out the memory.

His grip had tightened on her hand. She wanted to say so many things to him, but recalled Alana's advice to simply listen. "I was disappointed in a *major* way," he said. "And mad. I was trapped in medical purgatory, and there was absolutely nothing I could do about it. There'd been no operation, and what was worse, I have to go through the whole thing all over again when they do find me a liver."

He glanced up at her, and his intense inner struggle with self-pity was written on his face. "Anyway, here I am. Still waiting."

"All of us felt bad for you," Meg said softly. "I talked to your mother, and now more than ever, I think we need that family guest house."

"Maybe so. But now more than ever, I think she needs a home of her own. How's your search coming along? Any prospects yet?"

Crossing her fingers and hoping he didn't see how she was hedging, she mumbled, "Not yet." In truth, she hadn't looked at all. So many things were going on that she'd not done a thing about her promise to him.

"I don't want this Wish Foundation money to go to waste," Donovan insisted. "If anything, this check from JWC is what's keeping me from going nuts."

"How do you mean?"

"Because I know it's there. Because I know it can buy my mom and Brett a future. It was all I thought about when my head started to clear in ICU. I kept telling myself to hang on so that I could get well enough to get out of this place and take my mother to the house I'm going to buy for her."

Meg swallowed guiltily. She was holding up his dream by not following through with her promise to find a realtor and go house hunting. "Well, you keep getting stronger, all right? I swear I'm going to find some houses for you to pick from."

"Just think, I don't have to recuperate from transplant surgery before I buy, do I? All I have to do is survive until the next time." He looked directly into Meg's eyes. "If there is a next time."

That evening, as Meg wearily let herself into her house, her mother hurried up to hug her. "I've been waiting for you to get home. Guess what, honey? The Junior League board has approved your project. We're going to work on raising money to build a home away from home for patients' families. Isn't that exciting?"

# Thirteen

◈

MEG SET DOWN her purse and car keys on the marble-topped table in the spacious foyer. "The project's been approved? That's great, Mom. We need the house so much." Meg kept thinking about Mrs. Jacoby and all the parents like her.

"I knew you'd be pleased. It was your brainchild." Her mother hooked her arm through Meg's. "We'll have a meeting Friday morning with an architect. He's a relative of Betty Hotchkiss's and is willing to donate his services. That's the key, you know—to get as much donated as possible. I think it would be nice if you could attend the meeting."

"I'll be working at the hospital."

"You're only a volunteer. You may have to reexamine your priorities now."

Meg didn't want to reexamine her priorities. She wanted to be around the hospital. Around Donovan. "People are counting on me up in pediatrics."

"This idea was yours, and your presentation to the Junior League board was so persuasive. I naturally assumed you'd want to be a big part of it. I'm proud of you, Meg. This is such a good idea, but it will require a lot of work. We can do it if we all pull together."

Meg had assumed that once the Junior League took it over, she wouldn't be involved. She remembered the ideas she and Alana had joked about regarding fund-raising. "I had thought about a fund-raising letter," she said tentatively.

"A letter! We'll do many of them. You know, a project of this scope needs the support of the entire community. We have to get everyone involved, from schoolchildren to high-level politicians. However, if you have an idea for such a letter, go ahead and work it up."

Meg felt a growing respect for her mother. All her life, Meg hadn't taken her mother's charity work seriously. Perhaps it was because she was always going off to some luncheon or party, hardly *work* to Meg's way of thinking, but now Meg saw how significant all her mother's contacts were. Without the help of important Washington people, the project would never materialize.

"You're needed at the planning stages also, Meg. Your ideas are important," her mother said.

*My ideas?* Meg thought. All she had been interested in was a place near the hospital where Mrs. Jacoby could stay close to Donovan.

Her mother continued, "We'll be having a brainstorming session Sunday afternoon. I've invited some of the hospital personnel, several community and business leaders, and some politicians. I'm certain we'll select a special board of directors from this group, since they'll be people with a vested interest in our project. Each one of them has a special link to Memorial—a few have lost someone they loved."

Meg thought of Cindy's parents. Too bad they lived so far away. "Will big foundations support us?" Meg was thinking about Donovan's Wish money and the "invisible" One Last Wish Foundation. Perhaps it could be flushed out into the open and asked for a major donation. Perhaps she could learn the identity of JWC, maybe even meet the person who had written Donovan's letter and been responsible for authorizing his check.

"There's lots of competition for charitable dollars, but we have a very valid project that will benefit the whole community. I don't see how foundations and corporations can refuse. They require a special touch, however. Fortunately, some of the people attending Sunday's meeting have experience in that area."

"And you want me to attend that meeting?"

"Absolutely."

"How about my friend Alana? Her brother had a transplant."

"Bring them both. Your father also thinks we should ask Mrs. Jacoby. She's got a son in need of a transplant. Who better to speak up about the project?"

"Mom, thanks for all your help." The words sounded inadequate.

Her mom smiled. "I think our family is extremely blessed, Meg. Your father, myself, our children. I truly believe that giving something back to show appreciation for our blessings is our duty. I know you've had a rough year, but it does my heart good to see you pulling out of it."

*A rough year . . . you could say that,* Meg thought. And yet, her mother was right. Whole days now passed by when she didn't think about Cindy. A momentary twinge left her feeling disloyal, then the feeling passed. She had others to think about now. She had Donovan, and she wanted to keep him. More than anything in the world, she wanted him to live.

"Two million dollars, Alana! Mom said the architect estimates that the house will cost close to two million dollars. How can we raise that much money?"

"It is a lot." Alana was sitting out on the hospital patio, licking an ice-cream cone. "More than in this girl's piggy bank."

"We'll be old ladies by the time this house gets built."

"At least out of high school."

"You're not taking this seriously."

"Yes, I am. I just know it won't help to get all worked up about that sum of money. You've got to think in bite-size pieces." She took another lick off her cone. "All we need is two million people to give one dollar. Or one million people to give two dollars apiece. Or four big corporations to give five hundred thousand dollars each. Two million doesn't seem so overwhelming when you think of it that way."

Meg opened her mouth to argue, but stopped. Alana's logic made sense. "The other thing Mom told me was that the architect was concerned about the site, the place to build the house."

"Do they have a site?"

"Right now, land's pretty scarce around the hospital. Most of it's already been bought by developers, and it really is expensive. There's a place here on the Memorial property, but it's been designated for a new parking lot."

Alana wrinkled her nose. "A house for parents is more important than a parking lot."

"We know it, but the hospital board has to approve the change. It'll go into a committee for study—I swear, this is going to take forever." Feeling glum, Meg slouched in her chair.

"But it *will* happen," Alana assured her. "It may seem like it's taking forever, but one day, you'll look out across the grounds," she gestured with her arm, "and you'll see this wonderful house full of parents with kids up on our floor. And you and I will say, 'We helped get this house off the ground.'"

"Okay. I won't get too discouraged this early in the project. Will you and Lonnie be at the meeting Sunday?"

"We'll be there. You want to go to the mall with me tomorrow? I need something new to wear if I'm going to be with all those important people."

Meg shook her head. "I can't. I've already made plans." She didn't explain, even though Alana was looking expectant. How could she tell her that she was going house shopping? Especially when it was Donovan's secret?

"May I help you?" asked the woman behind the front desk of the real estate office when Meg entered.

Nervously, Meg licked her lips and smiled. She had spent two hours trying to make herself appear older than sixteen. She had selected her finest designer clothing and accessories and donned her best gold jewelry. She was glad that her mother had taught her how to dress for a strong first impression. While she certainly felt more comfortable in jeans, she knew the best way to be believed was to appear believable. "I have an appointment with Ms. George."

The receptionist buzzed an inner office, and soon a tall woman with blond hair came out to greet Meg. If she was surprised by Meg's youth, she didn't show it. Stepping into Ms. George's office, Meg took a seat on a sofa.

"I'm positive I can find you just the right home, Miss Charnell. After our phone discussion, I've chosen several houses I think you will find satisfactory," Ms. George said.

Meg cleared her throat. "As I told you, I'm doing this for a friend. He trusts my judgment for the preliminaries, but he'll be making the final choice."

"Don't think a thing about it. I understand completely. I've done many real estate transactions via third parties. Just last month, a wealthy foreign businessman sent his daughter to me. It seems that she'll be starting at Georgetown University in the fall, and he wanted her to buy herself a house near the campus rather than live in the dorms. It's not only a place for her to live, but an investment for him."

Meg returned the agent's cheerful smile. "You understand that my friend needs to be around the Memorial Hospital area."

"So you said." The agent frowned thoughtfully. "I must tell you that it won't be easy. That area rarely has houses on the market." She brightened. "But I have many alternatives to show you. Lovely homes that are only minutes from Memorial via the Beltway."

"Let's take a look," Meg said. "My friend wanted to get this house business settled as quickly as possible." She didn't add her deepest concern: *"Because he might not have too much longer to live."*

They spent several hours looking at prospective homes. Meg liked some, yet found only two she wanted to show to Donovan, and they weren't perfect. Frankly, she thought the residences were too far from Memorial in spite of their proximity to bus routes.

When they arrived back at the real estate office, Ms. George told her, "Don't be discouraged. Finding the right home takes time. It's not like buying a dress you can take back if you don't like it."

Meg agreed. "Keep looking, please. And call me anytime you think you have something to show me."

"I shall. Your friend won't be disappointed. We'll find something that's just right for him."

Meg drove home, disappointed that she hadn't done better in her search. She was feeling the pressure of time more acutely than ever. Donovan was stable at the moment, but she knew that could change in the blink of an eye. She gripped the wheel and prayed his health would hold until his dream was accomplished to buy his mother a home with his One Last Wish money.

# Fourteen

"How can I help?" Donovan asked once Meg explained her idea to him.

"As soon as Alana gets here, I want the three of us to work on a fund-raising letter together."

"What kind of a letter?"

"It was an idea I had when I heard all those people sharing ideas at Sunday's meeting. Everyone agrees that we need some letters to get public support. Did I tell you that several of the TV stations are carrying the story on their six o'clock news shows throughout the week?"

"My mom told me. She's pretty excited about the project. It's all she talked about when she visited me last night."

"So about the letter . . . I thought, 'Why not do

a letter from an actual patient? Someone who knows about the problem firsthand?' "

"You mean me?"

"Of course, I mean you. I had this idea because I saw how difficult it was on your mother and Brett having to be so far away from you."

"You mean something like JWC's letter?"

"Something like it, only different." Meg admitted that the One Last Wish letter and its personalized, informal feeling had impressed her. Surely, they could do something similar, except using it to ask for money instead of giving away money.

"It's a good idea, but I'm not much of a letter writer," Donovan said.

"That's why Alana and I are volunteering to help. If the three of us write one terrific letter, the board will have no choice but to use it. It'll be our contribution."

"Sounds all right to me. Who will you mail it to?"

"The new board for the project has a big mailing list of people who've been patients at Memorial, or who are known to give contributions to worthy causes—especially medical ones. This whole project is going to take off like a rocket."

"You really think the place is going to get built?"

"I do. First of all, we're naming it the Wayfarer Inn, a home away from home. Do you like it?"

"It sounds like a hotel."

"Oh, it'll be more than a hotel. It'll have ten to twelve bedrooms, a central kitchen, a playroom, a

TV room, a game room, laundry facilities, a library—" She paused to catch her breath. "And any family who has a child over here in Memorial for long-term treatment, like an organ transplant, can stay at the inn for only five dollars a night."

"I'm impressed," Donovan said.

"You're impressed with what?" asked Alana, breezing through the doorway.

"I'm impressed with the plans for the Wayfarer Inn."

Alana pulled up a chair alongside Meg's and sat down. "I'm so excited about the whole thing that I was awake half the night. Lonnie has a great idea—a fund-raising marathon."

"It works for me," Donovan replied.

"And did Meg tell you our ideas for the schools next year?"

"I haven't had a chance yet."

"So, tell me."

Meg moved forward. "We'll get kids in the elementary schools to bring a penny a day for a whole month to plop in jars in each classroom. If every kid brings just a penny a day, we'll collect a fortune."

"We figure every kid can afford a penny," Alana inserted.

"For the middle schools, we'll have walkathons and bake sales. In the high schools, we'll have highway holdups."

"Never heard of them. Are they legal?" Donovan asked.

"Sure are," Alana said. "Certain kids get official

badges to stand at busy intersections and hold buckets for motorists to toss in their pocket change. Everytime the light changes, there's a new crop of cars and a new source of coins."

"What else?"

"Well, we don't want you to think Meg and I have *all* the good ideas," Alana said. "The others at the meeting had a few too. In two weeks, the Junior League is planning a Moonlight on the Potomac cruise."

Donovan rolled his eyes. "That sounds pretty romantic—you know, not like mud wrestling or bowling for charity."

"You got something against romance?" Alana chided.

"Romance with a purpose," Meg insisted, swatting his arm playfully. "We get all these rich people out on a riverboat on the Potomac River, feed them, let them dance, then put on a presentation for the Wayfarer Inn and ask each person how much he or she wants to give."

"Notice we said, *how much*, not *if* they want to give."

"Sort of a captive audience out there on the river," Donovan observed.

"Exactly. Either they give or they swim home."

They shared a laugh over Meg's reasoning.

"Will you two be going on the cruise?" Donovan asked.

"Sure," Alana said. "Someone has to keep a check on donations."

"Who are you going to take?" Donovan's question was for both of them, but his eyes were on Meg.

"She'd like to take you, boy, but she's too slow in asking."

Meg felt her face turn beet red, and she shot Alana a glance that could kill.

"Are you inviting me?" Donovan wanted to know.

Meg straightened. "I was planning on it, but in my own time." No one mentioned what was on all their minds: In two weeks, he could be too sick to go.

"I accept," Donovan said.

"You do?"

"He does," Alana replied, standing. She brushed her hands together, as if dusting them off. "That was an easy matchup. Now, I'd better get to it and find myself a date. First person I'm asking is Carl Douglas, one fine hunk of man."

"Now that we have your social life settled, how about that letter?" Meg hauled Alana back to her chair.

"I was getting to that." Alana sat down, and Meg passed her a pencil and paper. "How should we start?"

"Donovan, if you could tell people one thing about how you feel concerning the Wayfarer Inn, what would it be?"

Sobered, he contemplated Meg's question. When he spoke, the words came from deep inside him. "Waiting for an organ transplant is truly hard work. It's hard not to get discouraged. Even harder when you get psyched up to go through the surgery and have a possible donation fall through. But I have to say that the hardest part of this whole ordeal is not being able to have your family near you while you're waiting.

"I'm seventeen and thought I was beyond the stage of needing my family close by. But I'm not. Sometimes, when I feel so low, I think it would take a crane to boost me over a curb, I need the closeness of my mom and kid brother. It's not that the hospital people aren't good to me—they are. But sometimes, more than anything in the world, I want to hold my mother's hand."

Donovan's voice had grown thick with emotion. Meg felt a lump in her throat. She had thought she understood Donovan's situation, but she hadn't. Not truly. She realized that her simple ability to come and go as she pleased, to be with her parents in her home, was something that she'd taken for granted. Donovan had no home, and his family was not able to help much because there was no place nearby for them to stay.

"That was pretty real, Donovan," Alana said, her voice sounding whispery. "If we can put that kind of emotion into a letter, I know we'll raise a ton of money."

He glanced away, obviously self-conscious. "It's common for little kids to want their mommies," he said. "I thought it might be more effective if people understood that big kids need theirs too." He offered a sheepish smile. "So, that was from the bottom of my heart. Now, on the lighter side, you can say that another reason for building the inn is to have access to a kitchen where my mom can bake up a batch of her special chocolate chip cookies. This hospital food gets boring."

"That request alone should bring in plenty of contributions," Meg joked.

"I already want to donate to the cause," Alana added. "Anyone who can bake chocolate chip cookies deserves a place to do it."

They worked for another hour, each making suggestions, but allowing Donovan to put his unique perspective into the letter above all else. When they were finished, Meg felt satisfied with the results. "I'll show this to Mom and Dad and see what they think," she said. "If they like it, we can get it out soon."

"I hope it helps," Donovan said.

"I know it will, because it came from your heart."

"That's true," he said. "Straight from my heart."

Once Alana had gone, Donovan took Meg's hand and sank back onto his pillow. He looked tired. "I appreciate all you're doing for me," he told her.

"It's for every kid stuck in long-term hospitalization," she said, but knew that he sensed the truth—it was mostly for him she was doing it.

"I'm going to do everything I can to stay well so that I can go on that cruise with you."

"You'd better. I'm counting on you."

"Unless a new liver comes along, that is."

"It's the only excuse I'll accept," she said. Then, on impulse, Meg bent, quickly kissed his cheek, and bolted from the room.

# Fifteen

"Meg, this is wonderful." Her mother put down the rough draft of Donovan's letter and wiped moisture from the corner of her eye. "It's so sensitive and heartfelt. I think you've done an excellent job. I'll present it to the board, and maybe we can get it mailed out before the cruise. I know it'll raise some money for our cause."

Her father took the letter and read it as he ate. They were having one of their rare dinners together, and Meg was actually appreciating their time with one another. "This is good," her father said. "I told you Donovan was a special kid."

"I'd like to take him on the cruise if you'll give him a pass from the hospital again," Meg said.

"To be honest, I'm planning on releasing him from Memorial."

"Is he well enough?"

"He's well enough to wait around his apartment as easily as at the hospital. Medically, Dr. Rosenthal has done all he can for him. Now, it's up to me and my team to find him a new liver. It's still his only recourse."

Meg felt nervous about having Donovan so far away from the hospital—and from her. "But what if you find a donor? Or what if he gets sick? His mother works all day—"

"He'll be on a beeper," her father interrupted gently. "If we get a compatible donor, he can be brought here by ambulance in no time at all. Same thing if he starts feeling bad. Calling for an ambulance is a decision he can make for himself if he gets sick and he's alone."

Meg was certain that Mrs. Jacoby wouldn't like leaving him alone day after day. "It just seems that he's safer in the hospital," she said.

"He's stable now, and there's nothing we can do for him at Memorial for the time being. Frankly, we need the beds for sicker patients." How sick did a person have to be? Meg wondered. Needing a new liver seemed to qualify in her mind. Her father reached over and squeezed her shoulder. "It'll be all right, Megan. It will be good for his morale to get out of the hospital for a while. I know what I'm doing."

Her father was right about the morale part. When she saw Donovan the next day, he was all smiles. "I'm blowing this place," he said. "Mom's coming to help me pack tonight after she gets off work."

"I'll drive you home."

"She was going to get us a cab."

"Why spend the money when I know the way?"

"You don't mind?"

"Of course not. Meg's Taxi, at your service."

"You'll come visit me?"

"Every chance I get." She watched him shuffle over to the dresser and remove clothing from the drawer. She realized how much she was going to miss stopping by his room every day. She told herself that this was good for him, but it was herself she was thinking about. "I'll call you during my breaks."

"I'd like that."

"And I can drive over this weekend."

"Mom'll fix us dinner."

"And in two weeks, we have the cruise."

"Don't worry. I'll be going." He came over to her and placed his hands on her shoulders. "Look, I'm scared about leaving Memorial too."

"I hope I'm not making you feel that way."

"You're not. According to Dr. Rosenthal, it's natural for me to be uneasy. As long as I'm here, I can ring for a nurse if I need anything. I know when I stay at home, I'll have to be on my own. Even though I'll have my medications and the phone close by, it's still scary. But I'd rather be scared than stuck here another day." He grinned down at her. "Besides, you should have heard Brett's voice when I told him on the phone I was coming home. He's planning some big surprise for me."

"I'll bet." She knew how much Brett had missed him. She was beginning to miss her sister, Tracy. Meg guessed that separation did make people long for each other. "Just stay well," she told Donovan.

"I'll do my best," he said. "Maybe next week, I can go see some of those houses you were telling me about."

"Maybe," Meg answered, wishing she had more choices to show him. "The agent's still working on it."

"Then, things are looking pretty bright, don't you think? We're helping to get contributions for the Wayfarer Inn, I'm shopping for a house for my mom—thanks to JWC—I'm getting out of Hotel Memorial, and I'll soon be going on a moonlight cruise with a pretty girl. Things don't look too bad at all to me."

*Except for your health*, Meg thought. She longed to share his enthusiasm, but she'd been with her father on that late-night run to Bethesda. She'd never told Donovan about it. But she had seen with her own eyes how quickly joy could turn into mourning.

"I didn't exaggerate one bit, did I? Isn't this place perfect?" Ms. George ushered Meg and Donovan through the front doorway of the old house. Her heels clicked across the hardwood floors, sending echoes off the walls. "I couldn't believe anything would actually become available in this neighborhood. As I told you on the phone, the elderly woman who owned it recently died in a nursing home. She had no relatives and left no will. She'd taken out a mortgage to help pay her nursing home bills, and when she died, the bank put the house up for sale."

Ms. George waved her hand. "I don't mean to rattle on about it, but when my friend at the bank called and told me about this house, I thought it sounded just perfect for you."

Meg glanced about the house with dismay. It looked run-down and smelled musty, of rooms too long closed up against fresh air and sunlight. "It's really old," she observed, filling in the silence.

"It was built in the 1890s. I know it needs work," Ms. George said hastily. "That's a big reason why the bank is selling it below market value. But its structure is sound, and you won't find craftsmanship like this anymore. Wallpaper, new paint, new appliances will fix the place up like new. I'm telling you, it's a real bargain."

Meg glanced at Donovan, who was taking his time touring the Victorian-era room. He stopped in front of the fireplace and ran his hand over the mantel. "This has been hand-carved," he said.

"There's another fireplace upstairs. Five bedrooms too." Ms. George chuckled. "I know that's far more space than you said you needed, but I figured I owed you right of first refusal on it."

Meg and Donovan exchanged glances. She

wished she could read his mind. Was he as disappointed in this house, as he'd been in the others she'd selected for him to see?

"The thing I thought you'd appreciate most was its proximity to Memorial Hospital," Ms. George continued. She turned toward the open front door with its beveled, stained-glass insets. "Only two blocks away."

"You said it's on a double lot?" Donovan asked.

"Yes, indeed." Ms. George fairly beamed. "Come through the kitchen."

Meg tagged behind the agent and Donovan through a swinging door. The kitchen looked bleak and cramped, in need of renovation. Ms. George led them out onto a back porch and pointed toward the backyard. "The bank hired a crew to mow and clear out the overgrowth, but see how generous the yard is?"

Meg saw that it sloped downward and a huge oak tree loomed in the back corner like a giant sentry. "Brett would have fun playing back there," she said, trying to sound upbeat.

"My mom loves Victorian houses," Donovan said. "She's always buying magazines about them. She wants a garden and lots of wildflowers on her lawn every spring."

"Come see the upstairs," Ms. George urged. "The staircase is solid cherry, and the newel post has a carved figurine—very unusual. There's a stained-glass window set over the stairwell too. It's a true antique."

As they climbed the stairs, the late-afternoon

sun slanted through the old window and peppered Donovan's shoulders and head with shades of red, yellow, and purple, making him look as if he'd stepped out of the past, from a time and place Meg had only read about. As they passed from room to room, Meg could see the beauty of the house beneath layers of grime and dust. Wainscoting, vaulted stenciled ceilings, rich old woods needing little more than lemon oil and buffing to make them gleam, caught her eye. "It is pretty," she whispered to Donovan as they circled the master bedroom.

"Our house in Virginia was an imitation of this," he said. "This is the real thing."

"Brett would be sliding down the banister every day."

"And I could have two rooms for myself. One to sleep in, one for my stereo gear." He walked around, touching the walls. "Mom could have an office of her very own, where she could help with the fund-raising effort for the Wayfarer Inn."

Meg thought that was a strong feature too. Mrs. Jacoby had become quite involved with the work of raising money for the inn. "Do you think you should look at some others?" Meg asked.

"No, this is the house I want for my mom," Donovan said, facing Ms. George. "How do I go about buying it?"

"I can have the paperwork started tomorrow. All I need is a down payment."

"I can write you a check right now. Tell me what else I have to do."

Meg was amazed that he'd made his decision so quickly. It was true that the house was in a perfect location, but she wanted it to be newer and more modern. While Donovan and the realtor discussed details, she formulated a plan to help spruce up the place. As she was driving him back to his apartment, she said, "We can paint it and clean it up. I know Alana will help if I ask her. There are others too up in pediatrics who will pitch in." She thought of all the nurses and technicians who cared about Donovan.

"I'd appreciate all the help I can get. I can do some of the work, but I know I can't do much. I don't have much energy these days."

Meg's heart constricted with his words. She wanted him to be well and healthy. "We can do it," she said cheerfully.

"I want my mom to see it at its best," he said. "But we can't take too much time fixing it up. I don't mean to sound ungrateful, but I have to think about getting it done quickly." He cut his eyes sideways. "Time is my enemy," he said softly.

Meg gripped the wheel, knowing what he said was true. "We'll get it done," she promised. If JWC could supply the money for fulfilling Donovan's dream, then the least she could do was help him present his dream in the best possible condition.

"It's a beautiful house, Meg and it's mine." He touched her hair, gently tucking it behind her ear. "All mine."

# Sixteen

❧

THUNDER RATTLED THE windows of the old house, and rain pelted the glass panes. "This is some storm," Alana exclaimed as she climbed down from a ladder with a bucket of paint. "I'm sure glad we're on the inside looking out."

Meg paused as she scraped peeling paint off of plaster walls. "Maybe we should take a break." The empty room amplified the sound of the pounding rain, making it difficult to hear the portable radio plugged in to the wall. She turned toward Donovan. He was sitting on a beanbag chair in the center of the room, watching them work. "Up for a snack?" Meg asked. "I've brought food in an ice chest I stashed in the kitchen."

"I'm okay," he insisted with a wave of his hand. "But you deserve a break."

"Thanks for the permission," Meg joked. She knew it was hard for him to sit and watch, even though it was all he had the strength to do. Meg had organized a crew, and over the past week, they had painted almost every room. Most of the day's volunteers had left before the heavy rain had started. Now the only ones left were Donovan; Alana; her boyfriend, Clark; Alana's brother, Lonnie; and Meg.

From upstairs, Meg heard the rumble of the floor polisher Lonnie was using. She hoped Lonnie's robust health encouraged Donovan. To look at Alana's well-muscled, broad-shouldered brother, it was difficult to believe he'd been in complete kidney failure. Surely, Donovan would rally physically in a similar way once he had his transplant, Meg told herself.

"I'll get the food," Clark said, taking the paint bucket from Alana. "Let's have an indoor picnic."

"Who cares if it's raining," Donovan said.

"No ants," Meg added.

Clark pushed aside the door separating the front room from the kitchen. "I'll help," Alana volunteered, tagging after him.

"It's not that heavy," Meg called.

"There's help, and there's help," Alana replied. "I'm thinking I should help with a kiss or two!"

"I understand." Meg laughed. She sat cross-legged on the floor beside Donovan and glanced about the partially painted room. "How's it look, boss?"

"You have paint chips stuck in your hair." Smiling, he picked off several. "And on your nose, your cheeks, your neck."

"I promise to get them all off before the cruise Saturday night. You are still coming, aren't you?"

"I rented a tux. Clark took me to the mall."

"That was nice of him."

"He's nice, that's true. And he and Alana really like each other."

His comment left Meg feeling uncomfortable. She wondered if he was remembering his former girlfriend and wishing he was with her. "They make a cute couple," Meg said.

"I'm looking forward to tomorrow night," he said.

"I found a great new dress," Meg told him.

"Just for me?" He grinned. "But then, I know how girls like to buy new clothes . . . any old excuse."

"Not 'just for you,'" she sniffed. "I needed something new." Ordinarily, she wouldn't have taken the time to go shopping. She'd tried on her best dress and discovered a lovely surprise—it was too large. When she'd gotten on the scale, she'd seen that she'd lost ten pounds since the beginning of the summer.

"'Needed,'" he echoed with a lift of his eyebrows. "You mean the way Brett needs another laser water pistol?"

"What happened to the one you gave him?"

"He shot one too many girls at summer school, so it was confiscated."

"He's a cute kid. I really like him."

Donovan sighed and surveyed the room. "I hope he likes this place. I hope it helps make up for our having to leave our old house and for life's being so hard." He tipped his head and looked deeply into Meg's eyes. "I appreciate all you've done for me," Donovan said. "I know you've spent a lot of time on this."

"I don't mind." She hadn't realized how much work went into buying a house until she'd helped him spend his Wish money. She'd had the water and electricity turned on. She'd selected and lugged all the paint and supplies to the house. "I want your mother to like it. The realtor was right—it needed paint and cleaning up. It really is a great house."

"Keeping it a secret from my mom's been hard, but time's almost up, isn't it?"

"I figure we'll be finished next week."

"Good. I'll feel like I can rest easier after I give her the keys."

A loud clap of thunder shook the windows. The lights flickered and then went off altogether. From the kitchen, Alana gave a squeal. Overhead, the drone of the polisher stopped abruptly. "Uh-oh," Meg said. "Looks like we're alone in the dark."

"Scared of the dark?" Donovan asked.

"Not a bit. Unless this house is haunted."

"I'll bet it is haunted. Just think—a long time ago, some sweet young thing sat in this very room—and some guy—put the moves on her."

"Maybe guys weren't like that once upon a time."

"Don't bet on it." He chuckled.

She felt his hand cover hers in the dark. His nearness and the husky sound of his voice in her ear were causing her pulse to flutter. "I've read that back long ago, girls and guys were never without chaperons."

"If chaperons were needed, then that just proves my point."

"We don't have a chaperon."

"Do you wish we did?"

"Why would we need one?" Her heart beat faster as his hand covered hers in the dark.

"We don't, I guess. You know what I wish?" His breath against her forehead made goose bumps skitter across her skin.

"That the lights would come back on?" She tried to joke, but her heart was thudding hard against her rib cage. She wanted him to hold her.

"I wish you could have known me before I got sick. I wish we could have dated when I was well."

Meg considered his words, while the rain splattered on the windowpanes. She doubted he would have even noticed her; she was plain and, until very recently, plump. "If you hadn't been sick, we would have never met," she concluded softly. "Why else would you ever have come to Washington?"

He was silent, but his hand moved slowly up her arm, to her face, where his fingertips glided along her hair. "You're right. Funny how good things can come out of bad."

Meg's mouth went dry, and she felt lightheaded from his nearness. More than anything, she wanted him to kiss her. "Is that what I am? A good thing?"

"You're the *only* thing that makes this whole crazy experience worth anything at all."

Suddenly, a flash of lightning lit the room, and for an instant, Meg saw Donovan's face etched in eerie brightness. She wanted to grab hold of him. Wanted to keep him from joining any ghosts that might be hovering over the house.

"Alana and Clark to the rescue!" Alana's voice called from the kitchen. The beam of a flashlight cut through the darkness. "Guess what Clark found in his car?" She flicked the light over Meg and Donovan. "It looks like you two don't need rescuing."

Meg scrambled to her feet. "No problem," she said. Her hands were trembling. "We're fine. How about your brother?"

"Lonnie?" Alana called. "You all right up there?"

"Fine, sis. I'm just sitting here in the dark with my trusty machine waiting for the electricity to roll."

"You want Clark to come up with the flashlight and lead you down to us? It might be a long wait."

"That would be nice."

Alana handed the flashlight to Clark. He flipped the beam toward the staircase. "I think we should pack it in for the night. I'll bet the electricity will be off for quite a while."

"Suits me," Donovan said, rising. "I wouldn't mind hitting the bed early. It's been a long day, and I've got some cruise to go on tomorrow night. I don't want to miss it."

"We're almost through here. We can finish things up next week," Meg added, still quivery with emotion.

Later, when the rain had stopped, Clark and Lonnie loaded up the cars while Donovan waited in the front seat of Meg's car. Meg and Alana stood together on the front porch. The fury of the storm had left the night freshly washed and sweet-smelling. "Sorry I came into the room when I did. I didn't mean to interrupt anything. My timing stinks," Alana said.

"I don't know what you mean. Donovan and I were just waiting for the lights to come back on. Nothing was going on."

"Sure. And I'm the Queen of England."

"It's true."

"Why don't you just admit it, girl? You're crazy about that boy."

"Because I'm not—not in that way."

"Listen, you can deny it with your mouth, but not with your heart. The way you feel about him is stamped all over you."

"I don't want to talk about this."

"Denying it won't make it go away. I know what you're thinking. You're thinking that it's stupid to love somebody who might up and die on you."

"Stop it. That's not true." Yet, Meg knew it was true. She didn't want to be in love with Donovan.

"Friends don't fib to friends," Alana said. "Don't be so scared of what you're feeling. If he does die, you won't be able to tell him how you feel. Don't let this opportunity get away from you."

Meg kept thinking about the loss—so senseless—of her friend Cindy. It had made her empty and afraid when she'd learned that Cindy had died. She couldn't go through something like that again. Admitting to herself that she loved Donovan would reopen wounds that still weren't healed, even though she knew she felt better after therapy. Why hadn't she listened to her father when he'd told her not to get emotionally involved?

*Because by the time he told me, it was too late.* Meg answered her own question. "I know you think you're helping me," Meg told Alana. "But I know what I feel. It's concern. It's overinvolvement with a patient. It's more than I should be feeling. But it isn't love. And Donovan isn't going to die either. The hospital will find him a donor, and my father will save him. That's his job, you know. He's saved others, and he'll save Donovan too."

Alana shook her head slowly. "Your father's a wonderful doctor and a fine man, but don't put that on him. It's not fair. He's not God, and he can't perform miracles."

"Are you saying that you think Donovan's going to die?"

"Not me. I've seen a miracle happen with my own brother. All I'm saying to you is to go with what you're feeling toward him and don't waste the chance to have something special because you're afraid."

"I'm not afraid," Meg snapped.

"We're *all* afraid," Alana said.

Meg could think of nothing to say to blot out the searing honesty of Alana's words. She wrapped her arms around herself and shivered. The rain had cooled the night air, but she knew that her shiver had come from inside herself, and had nothing whatsoever to do with the temperature. Not a single thing.

# Seventeen

MOONLIGHT CUT A wide swath across the peaceful, dark waters of the Potomac River. Standing on the deck of the huge riverboat, listening to the chug of the engine and watching moonbeams glitter on the water, Meg felt as if she'd been transported to another world. Behind her, from the ballroom, the music of an orchestra floated through the porthole.

"Having fun?" Donovan asked.

"The most. How about you?"

"I feel better tonight than I have in days. It's like I've been given a reprieve—you know, a delay in my sentence of sickness."

Alone with him in the moonlight, she felt as if his illness didn't exist. For just a little while, she could forget the real reason they were together on the boat. "I wish your mother had come," Meg said.

"I did everything to try and persuade her, but she didn't feel she belonged with these people. We're way out of this league financially. We're happy to get by, even though now the Wish money will help us. I've seen some people I recognize from newspapers and TV. I feel out of place myself."

"They're just people. And they all want to help build the Wayfarer Inn. We need them."

"I wonder if JWC is on this cruise. What do you think?"

Meg looked thoughtful. "I've seen the guest list, but no one with those initials stands out in my memory. Why does it matter?"

"Are you kidding? My mom will own a home because of JWC. I still can't get over being chosen to get all that money, so I'm really curious."

Meg straightened, feeling a slight prick of jealously because JWC had given Donovan something she could not. "No one I asked at the hospital ever heard of the One Last Wish Foundation," she said.

"I don't even know if JWC is a man or a woman."

"For that matter, you don't even know if that's the person's real initials. Maybe they're made up."

"But why?"

"Who knows?"

"Intimate strangers?" he offered.

She recalled their conversation—Donovan's explanation about how strangers could become linked by the intensity of a shared problem. She had no illness to share with him, as JWC had. "Maybe JWC only wants privacy. Rich people are like that sometimes."

"But I keep asking myself, 'Why me?' I'm so ordinary."

He wasn't ordinary to Meg, but she didn't tell him that. "If you ask me, I don't think JWC is playing fair."

"What do you mean?"

"Remaining anonymous is a cop-out. I think it's sort of cowardly to pass out money and then hide in the shadows. What's it prove? I mean, look at you. You'd like to say thank you, but how can you? And if JWC has so much money, then why not step forward and support our cause?"

Donovan shook his head slowly. "I don't know. In a way, what you're saying makes sense. I would like to meet the person who's been so good to me, but JWC must have big reasons for staying out of the spotlight. I'm not sure that if it were me, I wouldn't choose to do the same thing."

"How so?"

Donovan thrust his hands into the pockets of his tux and leaned against the ship's rail. "All those people inside are rich, and everybody knows it."

"That's one of the reasons they were invited."

"I know. They expect to be asked for charitable donations. Maybe some of them get jollies out of it because it makes them feel important. But when you do something for someone and expect nothing in return, it makes you feel good inside. It makes you feel ..." he searched for a word, "fulfilled. Doing something nice for someone in secret has its own reward. Maybe JWC knows that too."

Meg remembered how nice Donovan was to everyone on the pediatric floor. Why, the first time she'd met him, he'd been racing a kid in a wheelchair in spite of being so sick himself. And she thought of how different she herself was. Hadn't she become a candy striper because her father had coerced her into it? Helping others hadn't been something she'd longed to do, as it was for Donovan, or Alana.

Hadn't she spent over six months in mourning for her loss of Cindy without much concern for Cindy's parents? Had she called them, written them recently? No, she had not. And how about her own parents? How worried they must have been about her when depression had all but taken over her life.

*Losing Cindy hurt so much,* she told herself. But at what point had Cindy's death become a crutch that she used for an excuse to insulate herself from friendships and relationships that might cause her hurt? *Intimate strangers.* Did she want to go through the rest of her life never making lasting friendships again because she was terrified of being hurt? Had Alana been right when she'd challenged her the night before?

She felt Donovan's nearness, like a comforting

embrace. She cared for him so much. How could she have not understood all of this before? How could a sick, possibly dying boy, and a stranger who donated money anonymously, have given her so much? Why had she become interested in the Wayfarer Inn in the first place? Of course, there was a need for one, but as long as she was being brutally honest with herself, she had to admit that it was also because she felt competitive with JWC and wanted Donovan to feel indebted to her the way he did to JWC.

"You sure got quiet all of a sudden, Meg. Did I say something to upset you?"

Donovan's question snapped Meg out of her soul-searching. Quickly, she looked up at him. His face was softened by moonlight, and she felt something stir deep inside. A sleeping part of her was awakening as if from a long drugged sleep. "No, Donovan. You said some things that made me think."

"I did? Like what?"

"Like friends. We are friends, aren't we?"

He straightened and took her by the shoulders. "Since you've asked, Megan Charnell, you're the best friend I've ever had."

A warm melting sensation went through her.

"Look at them, will you, Clark? The two of them stand under a perfectly gorgeous moon *talking*! I swear, I've never known two people who spend so much time flapping their lips."

Meg and Donovan turned in unison toward Alana and Clark, who had come up beside them.

Alana stood with her hands on her hips, a look of pure frustration on her face.

Donovan suppressed a smile. "And what have you two been doing?"

"Not talking, that's for sure," Alana said with a saucy flip of her head.

Donovan glanced at Clark. Clark shrugged, spun Alana around, and kissed her firmly. When he pulled away, he said, "It's the only way I can shut her up."

"Shut me up!" Alana squealed.

"See you guys," Clark called over his shoulder, and darted across the moonlit deck. Alana followed, promising dire repercussions.

Watching them flee, Meg felt a wave of sadness come over her. She didn't want to feel sad. No matter what happened tomorrow, what became of her and Donovan, now it was safe and lovely. She turned back toward Donovan. "Do you suppose it's okay for best friends to give each other a kiss?"

He put his arms around her and drew her close. "I think it's required," he said. "Only for the sake of making the friendship stronger."

She slid her arms around him. "And only because we're best friends," she whispered, lifting her mouth to his. "And only to get Alana off our case."

He ducked his head downward. "Absolutely. That Alana can be so testy." His lips brushed hers, soft as a summer breeze.

# Eighteen

⌒⌒⌒

"THE FINAL TALLY is in, and we raised a bundle on the cruise last Saturday night," Meg's mother said as she hung up the phone in the kitchen. "That was the treasurer of our board, and she's very pleased. This, coupled with the letter you helped write, is really going to get us off to a fantastic start."

On her way out, Meg paused to hear her mother's enthusiastic report. "I'm glad. I know I had a wonderful time on the cruise."

"We'll have other fund-raisers. Right now, we're discussing a possible charity softball game. Initial inquiries to several big-name stars have been encouraging." She eyed Meg, who stood jangling her car keys. "I thought you had the morning off."

"I do. I'm taking Donovan and his mother someplace."

"Oh." Meg's mother started clearing off the kitchen counter. "I was hoping we could do something together. Shopping, lunch—we haven't done that once this summer."

Momentarily surprised by the wistful tone in her mother's voice, Meg stepped closer to the counter. "I already promised them," she said. This was the day that Donovan had chosen to take his mom to the house and tell her about the Wish money and how he'd spent it. Meg felt an edge of excitement. People had worked hard to get it ready. She wanted to tell her mom what was going on, but thought it best to keep Donovan's secret for a little while longer. Besides, the news would bring a barrage of questions from her mother, and she didn't have time to answer them. "Maybe we can go shopping tomorrow after I get off work," Meg suggested.

"I'll look forward to it."

Meg came around the counter and kissed her mother's cheek, causing her mother to glance at her with surprise.

"I just felt like it." Ever since the night of the cruise, she'd felt an affection for her parents she'd not experienced in a long time, and she was determined to make up to them for the strain her personal problems had caused her family. Now more than ever, Meg appreciated how they'd stood by her over the past months since Cindy's death and her difficult adjustment to it.

"Well, thank you. Anytime you feel like it is fine with me." She reached out and touched Meg. "You're doing better, aren't you?"

"You mean about Cindy? Yes, I think the worst is over."

"I'm glad. I've missed having my daughter around."

Meg gave her a quick hug and hurried out the door.

By the time Meg stopped her car in front of the old Victorian house, her palms were damp with nervous perspiration. From the backseat, she heard Mrs. Jacoby ask, "Donovan, what *is* going on? The two of you have been acting strange all morning."

Meg and Donovan exchanged glances in the front seat. "Just a little surprise Meg and I cooked up for you." Meg couldn't help noticing how tired and thin Donovan looked. A slight yellow cast tinged his skin. This was a moment he had been looking forward to for weeks, and she didn't want anything to ruin it for him.

"Where are we anyway?" Mrs. Jacoby asked, peering out the window. "My, what a lovely old house."

Donovan went around to his mother's door and offered his hand. "Come on. I want to show you the inside."

"Do you have permission? Is the owner home?"

Meg walked with them up onto the porch, trying to see the house through Mrs. Jacoby's eyes.

The front door with its leaded-glass panels sparkled in the morning sunlight. She remembered polishing each pane.

Donovan put the key into the lock, turned it, and swung open the door. "Come on, Mom. Look around and tell me if you like it."

"Donovan, are you sure—"

He pulled her in. "I'm sure."

The smell of fresh paint and lemon oil hung in the air, and sunlight streamed through the freshly washed front windows. Echoes sounded when they walked across the floor to the fireplace, now clean and empty of old ashes. Donovan ran his hand over the ornately carved mantel. "What do you think?" he asked.

His mother's gaze darted everywhere. "I think it's the most beautiful house I've ever seen. Who owns it?"

Meg stepped back, lingering near the entrance. She wanted them to have this special moment, yet felt that she would burst if Donovan didn't tell his mom the truth right away.

He crossed to his mom and took both her hands in his. "I want you to know how much what you did means to me."

"What did I do?"

"You sold our house and moved us here just so I could be near Memorial and have the chance for a transplant."

She shook her head. "It was your best chance, and I never thought twice about it. You're my son, and I love you. It was much harder on Brett than on me, although I think even he's adjusted."

"Still, I know what our home meant to you."

"It was old and needed repairs." She was obviously flustered by his words.

"It was our home," Donovan insisted.

"Well, if you brought me here to show me how beautiful a house can be, you've succeeded. I think this one is exquisite."

"You haven't even seen the upstairs yet," Meg blurted out.

Mrs. Donovan turned to her and smiled. Her eyes narrowed. "What have you two cooked up?"

Meg gave Donovan a helpless shrug, and he held up the house keys, opened his mother's hand and settled them in her palm. "It's yours, Mom. This house is yours—ours really. It's a present."

Her bewildered expression turned skeptical. "Now, Donovan, you can't expect me to believe that someone *gave* us this house."

"Believe it. It's a long story, and I'm going to sit right here in the middle of the floor and tell you all about it, but first, look at this." He reached into his back pocket and pulled out a folded manila envelope. Meg knew that inside was the deed to the house.

As Mrs. Jacoby read the legal document, the expression on her face turned from doubt to shock to stunned disbelief. "But how—?" Her voice cracked.

Donovan said, "I bought it for you and Brett. I

want you to have a home again. To make up for the other one."

"But—"

He shook his head. "In a minute." He opened his arms. Meg watched as his mother slid into them. Sunlight washed over them, bright and golden like a soft embrace. Meg blinked back tears as she heard Mrs. Jacoby begin to weep softly in her son's arms. "I love you, Mom," he said. "I love you."

It took over an hour for Donovan and Meg to explain about the One Last Wish Foundation and for Mrs. Jacoby to begin to believe them. She had many questions, most of which neither of them could answer, but Donovan did have the original letter and a copy of the check that Meg had made on the hospital's copy machine. Those things and the deed to the house were the only proof they could offer. In the end, it was enough.

Mrs. Jacoby went over every inch of the house, exclaiming over details that had escaped Meg even though she'd helped paint the whole thing. The size of the house almost overwhelmed Mrs. Jacoby, but she made plans for each room. They might have stayed longer, but Donovan wasn't feeling well, so Meg drove them back to the apartment.

Mrs. Jacoby chattered nonstop all the way. "Maybe we can arrange to move next weekend. I'll give notice to the landlord. I can rent a trailer. Do you think some of the people who helped you fix

the place up would help us move? I can't pay any-
body, but I could make a big pot of chili . . ."

Meg saw that Donovan was pleased, but also
tired. He leaned back against the car seat on the
long drive and closed his eyes. Meg let them off,
promising to call later. "I have my own mother to
tell," she told them. "Once she finds out I worked
so hard on your house, she may put me to work
on ours." She made a face that caused Mrs. Jacoby
to laugh, and waved good-bye.

Once she returned home, she found her mother
relaxing by the pool. "Back so soon?" her mom
asked.

"Donovan wasn't feeling well, so we cut it
short."

"Cut what short?"

Meg dragged a patio chair over and sat down
and proceeded to tell her mother the whole story.
When she finished, her mother stared at her in-
credulously. "I can't believe it," she said.

"I'm sorry I couldn't mention the One Last
Wish Foundation and the mysterious JWC before,
but it was Donovan's money, and he asked me to
keep it a secret until his mom got the house."

"Does your father know?"

"No, not even Daddy."

"And the two of you pulled this off all by your-
selves?"

"Yes," Meg confessed. "Are you mad at me?"

"Mad? I'm impressed!" Her mother's face broke
out in a generous smile.

"You are?"

"Your ingenuity is overwhelming."

"It is?"

"Meg, I think what you did is wonderful. I want you to start at the beginning and tell me the whole story all over again. Every detail—don't skip a thing. Then, I'm going to begin checking into this One Last Wish Foundation. I'd say they need to be approached for a *major* donation to the Wayfarer Inn."

Meg stared at her mother open-mouthed. "Why, that's exactly what I wanted to do!" she cried. "They should give to our cause."

Her mother smiled more broadly. "Like mother, like daughter," she quoted, then leaned forward, her eyes twinkling. "Scary, isn't it?"

They spent the afternoon talking and laughing as Meg told stories of her adventures as a candy striper. It was after six before her mother realized that they needed to start dinner. "Your father promised to be home tonight."

"Maybe we should go out to eat," Meg suggested. "Daddy hasn't taken the two of us out to eat in ages."

"Good idea. I think we should both dress and pounce on him the minute he comes in the door. I mean, how could he possibly refuse an invitation from two gorgeous women like us?"

The electronic ring of the phone interrupted Meg's reply. She tensed. Years of hearing the phone ring at dinnertime meant only one thing. Her father had an emergency and wouldn't be home for dinner. She tried not to feel resentful.

Her mother picked up the receiver. Her smile quickly faded as she spoke to Meg's father, and when she hung up, Meg braced herself for bad news.

"It's Donovan," her mother said. "He's just been brought into emergency, and he's unconscious."

# Nineteen

MEG FELT MISPLACED sitting in the familiar surroundings of Memorial. She wasn't a candy striper this time. She was a visitor. A watcher. One who waited for news about someone who was critically ill. She felt helpless.

Her mother sat in a corner with Mrs. Jacoby, holding her hand and consoling her. Brett was slumped in another chair, staring down at his lap; his legs dangled, still too short to touch the floor. The sight of him looking so small and lost in the ICU waiting room caused a lump to lodge in her throat. He looked over at her forlornly. "Donovan fell down on the floor," he said. "There was blood."

Meg slid over to sit next to the boy and put her arm around him. "I'm sorry, Brett. The doctors are trying to fix him up right now. Think about him getting better again."

"Is your daddy going to get him his new liver now?"

Sadness almost overwhelmed Meg. She knew that Donovan had been delegated a Status 9—the highest priority for transplantation—but she didn't know if the nationwide appeal for a liver had been answered. "I know my daddy's trying his very best," she told Donovan's sad little brother.

"The last time Donovan got real sick, Mommy told me that he might have to go to heaven. But he got better and got to come home. Will he have to go to heaven if your daddy can't find him a new liver?"

His questions, his innocence tore at her heart. Yet, his mother had discussed the possibility of Donovan's dying, so Meg figured that it would be cruel to gloss over the child's concerns. Still, she could hardly face the thought herself. "I-I don't know. Maybe." She turned her head and fought for control.

"He can have my liver," Brett said. "I never liked liver much anyway."

His cockeyed view of the situation brought Meg a brief smile. "Sorry, but one liver to a customer. You still need yours."

She heard someone rush into the room and looked up to see Alana, Clark, and Lonnie. They swiftly surrounded Meg and Brett. "Mrs. Vasquez called and told me. Oh, Meg, I'm so sorry."

"It stinks," Clark mumbled. "We just returned his tux on Monday. He didn't feel good, but I didn't think much about it. He never feels really good."

"I think he was holding on just so he could get the house finished," Meg said, realizing that was probably the truth. Any mention of being sick, and he would have been put back into the hospital immediately. "Turning over those keys to his mom was everything to him."

"Don't give up hope," Lonnie said. "I know what it's like to lie in a hospital bed and think life's over, then to get a reprieve. It can happen for Donovan too, if they only find him a donor."

Meg hung on to Lonnie's words as if they were a lifeline. *If they only find him a donor.* Suddenly, she wanted to see Donovan and touch him. Meg moistened her lips and stood. "Will you all wait here with Brett? I'll be back soon."

Clark eased into her vacated chair. "Hi, Brett, my man. I'm Clark, and I know your brother and we are pals."

Meg left the waiting room, went to the elevators, and punched the button that would take her to her dad's office. She had no reason to even hope that he was there, but she wanted him to be. She wanted to talk to him, wanted to hear straight from him how the search was going.

Because it was late, the halls were ghostly quiet. She walked swiftly down the long corridor and stopped in front of her dad's office door. She muttered a quick prayer, turned the knob, and stepped inside. "Daddy?" she said.

He swiveled the chair slowly to face her. "Hi, Meggie."

Again, she felt coldness clutch her heart. "Why aren't you down prepping for OR?"

"They just called me from the lab. Donovan's in kidney failure."

Meg's knees felt wobbly. She crouched in front of her father's chair and gazed up at him. "So, will you have to do a kidney transplant too?"

He didn't answer right away, but took a deep and shuddering breath. "There won't be any transplant. We've run out of time."

She heard the sharp intake of her own breath. "Is he—is he—?"

Her father shook his head. "Not yet. I was just sitting here figuring a way to go down and tell his family." He looked at her. "And you."

It dawned on her that her father was truly sad. What good was all the technology if it couldn't come through when it was needed? "Does Donovan know?"

"He's semiconscious, but I don't know if he's aware of what's happening. I don't think so. He'll go to sleep and slide from this world into the next. I can't stop him."

Meg had passed from acute pain into numbness. The pool of light from the lamp shone directly down on her father's hands, clasped in his lap. His fingers were long and tapered, spotlessly clean, smelling faintly of antiseptic soap. *Surgeon's hands. Hands that healed.* It was as if she were seeing them for the first time.

His hands were beautiful, and they had the power to transplant life from one human being into another. And yet, now, for all his knowledge, for all his ability and surgical skill, his hands could do nothing. He had the power to sustain life, but not to restore it.

She stared at her own hands too. Smaller than his, with a few stubborn flecks of paint embedded under her nails. She thought of Alana's hands, dark and nimble. She thought of all the hands that had reached out, that were still reaching out to Donovan and his family. Human hands, helping, healing, giving. Perhaps in the long run, that's what life was truly all about—helping one another.

Meg reached out and covered her father's hands with hers. "We broke the rules, didn't we, Daddy? We got too involved."

He nodded. "I'm afraid so, Meggie."

"Can I see him alone? Just for a minute while you go tell Brett and his mother?"

He answered by taking her hand and leading her out of his office.


ICU was quiet and dark except for the lonely vigil of beeping machines and glowing monitors. On the bed, Donovan twitched and tossed restlessly, as if struggling to remain in place. Tubes and wires protruded from every part of his body. Meg stared down at him, thinking, *He's tethered—*

*these lines hold him to the bed.* If they weren't in place, would he float away?

She felt detached, like an alien seeing something that made no sense in her world of health and wellness. Sickness she had seen, but death? Death wore a different face.

"Donovan, it's me, Meg. I-I want you to know I'm here with you." She had no way of knowing if he heard her, or even remembered her.

"Cold," he mumbled. "So cold."

His discomfort angered her, and she looked about for another blanket with which to cover him. There wasn't one. She could go to the nurses' station and ask for one, but she couldn't bear to leave him even for a minute. She had so little time as it was.

The curtain in front of the glass partition was pulled back, and she could see a nurse bent over a chart, dutifully filling it in. A glass wall and twenty yards separated them. It may as well have been a chasm. Meg couldn't catch her eye.

"Cold," Donovan mumbled through chattering teeth.

Making up her mind what to do, Meg reached over and jerked the curtain across the glass window, sealing herself and Donovan off from the main desk. Very carefully, she moved aside wires and tubes, and gently, she crawled into the bed beside him so that his back was resting against the front of her body.

She realized she was breaking all the rules, but it didn't matter. He needed her. With great care, she slipped her arms around him and held him close.

She willed the warmth of her body to seep into his, hoping he might somehow absorb a portion of her life into himself. She would gladly give a few of her years to him. "I'm here, Donovan," she whispered against his neck. "Right here."

His trembling seemed to stop, and after a few minutes, his body seemed more relaxed. She hugged him tighter, filling her arms with the weight of him, and her memory with his smile. Tears slipped down her cheeks.

With one hand, she stoked his hair. "When you get where you're going," she said into his ear, "please don't forget me. And once you're there, look for a friend of mine. Her name is Cindy, and you'll like her. Trust me."

She whispered his name like a prayer, "Oh, Donovan. Oh, Donovan. Oh, Donovan."

# Twenty

MEG STOOD AT the top of the staircase and looked down at the whirlwind of activity below. Carpenters were hammering boards, putting the finishing touches on a sun deck and a doorway that had been added on to the old Victorian house. Painters and decorators hurried from room to room behind her, dragging bolts of cloths and cans of touch-up paint. She heard her mother's voice call out, "Hurry up! The reporters and TV people will be here in less than an hour."

"Where do you want this tray of hors d'oeuvres?" another voice yelled from the kitchen.

"Put it in the fridge, and don't forget to take the others out of the oven," Mrs. Jacoby answered. She was standing on a ladder, held steady by

Alana, and hanging a plaque above the mantel, next to an oversize rendering of the Wayfarer Inn.

Meg knew the inscription on the plaque by heart, for it had been a gift to Mrs. Jacoby from all the candy stripers who'd worked together the previous summer. It was dedicated to Donovan's memory. She still couldn't believe it had been eight months since he'd died. At the time, she didn't believe she'd ever get over it, but although she still missed him terribly, the sharp pain of loss gradually had turned into a dull ache over the months.

She was positive that her involvement in the renovation of the house had made the time pass more quickly. She remembered with perfect clarity the day Mrs. Jacoby had come to her and her mother and asked, "May I talk to you about something?"

Donovan's mother had looked pale and borne the marks of her grief. His final days in ICU had still been fresh. "It's about the house," Mrs. Jacoby had said once Meg's mother had served them tea by the pool.

"Is something wrong with it?" Meg had asked.

"I can't live there."

Meg had been dumfounded. "Why not? Donovan wanted you to have it. It meant so much to him."

"I can't live there knowing so many parents such as myself have no place to stay when their children are in Memorial waiting for transplants."

"We're working as fast as we can to raise funds

for the Wayfarer Inn," Meg's mother had said. "It's going well, but these things take time."

"That's just the point. So many of those kids don't have time to wait. I have an idea—a way to help out." That day, she had outlined a plan to renovate her house, add necessary rooms, and open the house up as a temporary inn until the other could be built. She'd said that she and Brett would live there and be a source of support for parents whose kids were facing transplantation. "It seems so logical," she had added, after presenting her plan. "Donovan chose that house because of its proximity to the hospital. Volunteers can help me. We can cook and keep the rooms neat and baby-sit younger siblings. I've thought about it very carefully, and it's what I want to do."

In the end, the board of the League had thought it an excellent idea. They had allocated money for the renovation and appointed Mrs. Jacoby coordinator of the Wayfarer Inn, with the offer of extending the job to the new house once it was built. Meg had been pleased for her. It was something Mrs. Jacoby obviously wanted to do, and it seemed to give her a new lease on life.

Now, in less than an hour, journalists and TV anchors from Washington and Virginia would be showing up for the formal dedication of Wayfarer One. Meg stepped aside as a decorator hustled past, juggling rolls of wallpaper.

"You must be very proud," she heard a familiar voice say.

Meg turned and saw Mrs. Vasquez standing

next to her. "I didn't have too much to do with all this. It was Mrs. Jacoby's idea."

"I know how you've helped," the nurse insisted. "And I've seen copies of the letter you and Alana helped Donovan write. It's raising a lot of money for the cause."

"We're still a long way from building the main house."

"I've heard about a year. That's not so long."

Meg shrugged. "I'll be a senior by then."

"Will you work at the hospital next summer?" Mrs. Vasquez asked.

"I'm not sure." Meg wasn't sure she could go through another summer like the last one. How did long-time nurses like Mrs. Vasquez manage it year after year, caring for people who sometimes didn't get well?

"You want to know something?" Mrs. Vasquez asked.

"What?"

"You've really got a knack for medicine."

Meg stared at her in amazement. "Who, me?"

"I didn't always think that," the nurse continued. "When you first appeared on the floor I thought, 'This one will be gone by the end of the week.' But you fooled me. You not only stayed, you exhibited a real gift for doctoring."

"A gift? Me?"

Mrs. Vasquez laughed. "Don't sound so shocked. I've been in this business for over twenty years, so I've seen plenty of professionals—and believe me, not all of them should be in the business. No, true medicine requires the gift of caring. Your father has it. And from what I've seen, you do too." The nurse patted her arm. "For what it's worth, you might think about becoming a doctor. I know you'd make a good one."

Meg let Mrs. Vasquez give her a quick hug, then watched her hurry away. She mulled over the conversation. A doctor? Impossible!

"Are you going to stand there gawking all day, or are you going to come down here and give us a hand?" Alana called up to Meg from below.

"I'm coming," Meg called back. She took one final look at the upstairs area and at the stained-glass window set in the stairwell. The beautiful colors spilled over the landing and brought back the memory of the first day she and Donovan had toured the house. She felt his presence. Certainly, he was with them this day. As was the secretive JWC, whose identity remained a mystery despite her mother's efforts to ferret out information.

Meg knew that Donovan would be proud of what was going on in his house. She bounded down the stairs, dodging a man tacking down new carpet. Meg knew she'd never be able to give large sums of money to people in need, but she did have other things to offer. "Hey, Alana," Meg shouted as she reached the floor. "I've been think-ing . . . maybe we could go to med school to-gether? What do you think about a career in pediatrics?"

*Dear Reader,*

$\mathcal{F}$or those of you who have been longtime readers, I hope you have enjoyed this One Last Wish volume. For those of you discovering One Last Wish for the first time, I hope you will want to read the other books that are listed in detail in the next few pages. From Lacey to Katie to Morgan and the rest, you'll discover the lives of the characters I hope you've come to care about just as I have.

Since the series began, I have received numerous letters from teens wishing to volunteer at Jenny House. That is not possible because Jenny House exists only in my imagination, but there are many fine organizations and camps for sick kids that would welcome volunteers. If you are interested in becoming such a volunteer, contact your local hospitals about their volunteer programs or try calling service organizations in your area to find out how you can help. Your own school might have a list of community service programs.

Extending yourself is one of the best ways of expanding your world . . . and of enlarging your heart. Turning good intentions into actions is consistently one of the most rewarding experiences in life. My wish is that the ideals of Jenny House will be carried on by you, my reader. I hope that now that we share the Jenny House attitude, you will believe as I do that the end is often only the beginning.

*Thank you for caring.*

You'll want to read all the ONE LAST WISH
BOOKS BY BESTSELLING AUTHOR

*Let Him Live*

*Someone Dies, Someone Lives*

*Mother, Help Me Live*

*A Time to Die*

*Sixteen and Dying*

*Mourning Song*

*The Legacy: Making Wishes Come True*

*Please Don't Die*

*She Died Too Young*

*All the Days of Her Life*

*A Season for Goodbye*

*Reach for Tomorrow*

$\mathscr{I}$F YOU WANT TO KNOW MORE ABOUT MEGAN,

BE SURE TO READ

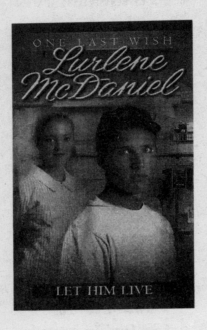

ON SALE NOW FROM BANTAM BOOKS
0-553-56067-0

Excerpt from *Let Him Live* by Lurlene McDaniel
Copyright © 1993 by Lurlene McDaniel

Published by Bantam Doubleday Dell Books for Young Readers
a division of Random House, Inc.
1540 Broadway, New York, New York 10036

$\mathcal{B}$eing a candy striper isn't Megan Charnell's idea of an exciting summer, but she volunteered and can't get out of it. Megan has her own problems to deal with. Still, when she meets Donovan Jacoby, she find herself getting involved in his life.

Donovan shares with Megan his secret: An anonymous benefactor has granted him one last wish, and he needs Megan's help. The money can't buy a compatible transplant, but it can allow Donovan to give his mother and little brother something he feels he owes them. Can Megan help make his dream come true?

*"When I first got sick in high school, kids were pretty sympathetic, but the sicker I got and the more school I missed, the harder it was to keep up with the old crowd,"* Donovan explained. *"Some of them tried to understand what I was going through, but unless you've been really sick . . ."* He didn't finish the sentence.

*"I've never been sick,"* Meg said, *"but I really do know what you're talking about."*

*He tipped his head and looked into her eyes. "I believe you do."*

$\mathcal{I}$F YOU WANT TO KNOW MORE ABOUT
KATIE AND JOSH, BE SURE TO READ

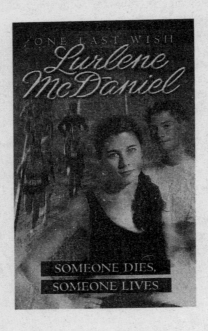

ON SALE NOW FROM BANTAM BOOKS
0-553-29842-9

Excerpt from *Someone Dies, Someone Lives* by Lurlene McDaniel
Copyright © 1992 by Lurlene McDaniel

Published by Bantam Doubleday Dell Books for Young Readers
a division of Random House, Inc.
1540 Broadway, New York, New York 10036

$\mathcal{K}$atie O'Roark feels miserable, though she knows she's incredibly lucky to have received an anonymous gift of money. The money can't buy the new heart she needs or bring back her days as a track star.

A donor is found with a compatible heart, and Katie undergoes transplant surgery. While recuperating, she meets Josh Martel and senses an immediate connection. When Katie decides to start training to realize her dream of running again, Josh helps her meet the difficult challenge.

Will Katie find the strength physically and emotionally to live and become a winner again?

*From the corner of her eye, Katie saw a boy with red hair who was about her age. He stood near the doorway, looking nervous. With a start, she realized he was watching her because he kept averting his gaze when she glanced his way. Odd, Katie told herself. Katie had a nagging sense she couldn't place him. As nonchalantly as possible, she rolled her wheelchair closer, picking up a magazine as she passed a table.*

*She flipped through the magazine, pretending to be interested, all the while glancing discreetly toward the boy. Even though he also picked up a magazine, Katie could tell that he was preoccupied with studying her. Suddenly, she grew self-conscious. Was something wrong with the way she looked? She'd thought she looked better than she had in months when she'd left her hospital room that afternoon. Why was he watching her?*

Katie is also featured in the novels *Please Don't Die, She Died Too Young,* and *A Season for Goodbye.*

𝒯F YOU WANT TO KNOW MORE ABOUT SARAH,

BE SURE TO READ

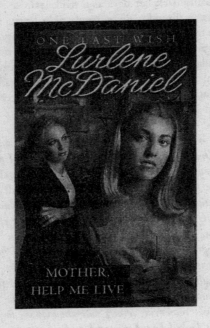

ON SALE NOW FROM BANTAM BOOKS
0-553-29811-9

Excerpt from *Mother, Help Me Live* by Lurlene McDaniel
Copyright © 1992 by Lurlene McDaniel

Published by Bantam Doubleday Dell Books for Young Readers
a division of Random House, Inc.
1540 Broadway, New York, New York 10036

Sarah McGreggor is distraught when she learns she will need a bone marrow transplant to live. And she is shocked to find out that her parents and siblings can't be donors because they aren't her blood relatives. Sarah never knew she was adopted.

As Sarah faces this devastating news, she is granted one last wish by an anonymous benefactor. With hope in her heart, she begins a search for her birth mother, who gave her up fifteen years ago. Sarah's life depends on her finding this woman. But what will Sarah discover about the true meaning of family?

*Didn't the letter from JWC say she could spend it on anything she wanted? What could be more important than finding her birth mother? What could be more important than discovering if she had siblings with compatible bone marrow? Her very life could depend on finding these people. Sarah practically jumped up from the sofa. "I've got to go," she said.*

$\mathcal{I}$F YOU WANT TO KNOW MORE ABOUT ERIC,

BE SURE TO READ

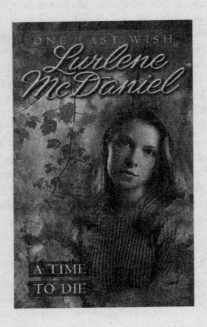

ON SALE NOW FROM BANTAM BOOKS
0-553-29809-7

Excerpt from *A Time to Die* by Lurlene McDaniel
Copyright © 1992 by Lurlene McDaniel

Published by Bantam Doubleday Dell Books for Young Readers
a division of Random House, Inc.
1540 Broadway, New York, New York 10036

*S*ixteen-year-old Kara Fischer has never considered herself lucky. She doesn't understand why she was born with cystic fibrosis. Despite her daily treatments, each day poses the threat of a lung infection that could put her in the hospital for weeks. But her close friendship with her fellow CF patient Vince and the new feelings she is quickly developing for Eric give her the hope to live one day at a time.

When an anonymous benefactor promises to grant a single wish with no strings attached, Kara finds a way to let the people who have loved and supported her throughout her illness know how much they mean to her. But will there be time for Kara to see her dying wish fulfilled?

*"What am I going to do about you, Kara?"*

*Eric's tone was subdued and so sincere that his question caught her by surprise. "What do you mean?"*

*"I can't stay away from you."*

*"You seem to be doing a fine job of it," she said quietly, but without malice.*

*"I know it seems that way, but you don't know how hard it's been."*

*She was skeptical. "We just danced together, but after tonight, how will it be between us? Will you still ignore me in the halls? Will you duck into the nearest open door whenever you see me coming?"*

*He turned his head and she saw his jaw clench. She thought he might walk away, but instead he asked, "What's between you and Vince?"*

$\mathcal{I}$F YOU WANT TO KNOW MORE ABOUT MORGAN,

BE SURE TO READ

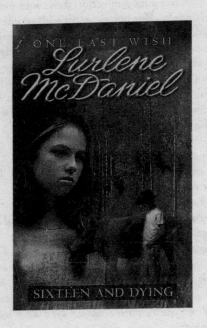

ON SALE NOW FROM BANTAM BOOKS
0-553-29932-8

Excerpt from *Sixteen and Dying* by Lurlene McDaniel
Copyright © 1992 by Lurlene McDaniel

Published by Bantam Doubleday Dell Books for Young Readers
a division of Random House, Inc.
1540 Broadway, New York, New York 10036

*I*t's hard for Anne Wingate and her father to accept the doctors' diagnosis: Anne is HIV-positive. Seven years ago, before blood screening was required, Anne received a transfusion. It saved her life then, but now the harsh reality can't be changed—the blood was tainted. Anne must deal with the inevitable progression of her condition.

When an anonymous benefactor promises to grant Anne a single wish with no strings attached, she decides to spend the summer on a ranch out west. She wants to live as normally as she possibly can. The summer seems even better than she dreamed, especially after she meets Morgan. Anne doesn't confide in Morgan about her condition and doesn't plan to. Then her health begins to deteriorate and she returns home. Is there time for Anne and Morgan to meet again?

*Fearfully, Anne stared at her bleeding hand.*

*Morgan reached beneath her, lifted her, and placed her safely away from the hay and its invisible weapon. "Let me see how bad you're cut."*

*"It's nothing," Anne said, keeping her hand close to her body. "I'm fine."*

*"You're not fine. You're bleeding. You may need stitches. Let me wipe it off and examine it."*

*Her eyes widened, reminding him of a deer trapped in headlights. "No! Don't touch it!"*

*"But—"*

*"Please—you don't understand. I—I can't explain. Just don't touch it." Wild-eyed, panicked, she spun, and clutching her hand to her side, she bolted from the barn.*

*Dumbfounded, Morgan watched her run back toward the cabin.*

# *Y*OU MAY ALSO WANT TO READ

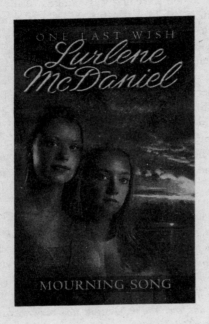

## ON SALE NOW FROM BANTAM BOOKS
### 0-553-29810-0

Excerpt from *Mourning Song* by Lurlene McDaniel
Copyright © 1992 by Lurlene McDaniel

Published by Bantam Doubleday Dell Books for Young Readers
a division of Random House, Inc.
1540 Broadway, New York, New York 10036

*I*t's been months since Dani Vanoy's older sister, Cassie, was diagnosed as having a brain tumor. And now the treatments aren't helping. Dani is furious that she is powerless to help her sister. She can't even convince their mother to take the girls on the trip to Florida Cassie has always longed for.

Then Cassie receives an anonymous letter offering her a single wish. Dani knows she can never make Cassie well, but she is determined to see Cassie's dream come true, with or without their mother's approval.

*Dani had rehearsed the speech so many times that even she was beginning to believe it. "It's as if you're supposed to do this. While we don't know who gave you the money for a wish, I think you should use it to get something you've always wanted. Listen, even a trillion dollars can't make you well, but the money you've gotten can help you have some fun. I say let's go for it! You deserve to see the ocean, whether Mom agrees or not. I'm going to help you make your wish come true."*

*I*F YOU WANT TO KNOW MORE ABOUT RICHARD
HOLLOWAY AND JENNY CRAWFORD,
BE SURE TO READ

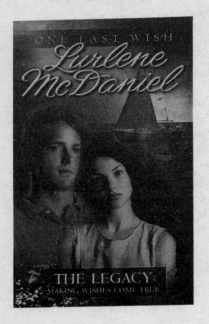

ON SALE NOW FROM BANTAM BOOKS
0-553-56134-0

Excerpt from *The Legacy: Making Wishes Come True* by Lurlene McDaniel
Copyright © 1993 by Lurlene McDaniel

Published by Bantam Doubleday Dell Books for Young Readers
a division of Random House, Inc.
1540 Broadway, New York, New York 10036

$\mathcal{W}$ho is JWC, and how was the One Last Wish Foundation created? Follow JWC's struggle for survival against impossible odds and the intertwining stories of love and friendship that developed into a legacy of giving. And discover the power that one individual's determination can have, in this extraordinary novel of hope.

"I had my physician call the ER doctor and afterward, when we discussed their conversation, he suggested that I get her to a specialist as quickly as possible."

"A specialist at Boston Children's," Richard said with a nod. "What kind of specialist?"

"A pediatric oncologist."

Before Richard could say another word, Jenny's grandmother spoke. "A cancer specialist," Marian said, her voice catching. "They believe Jenny has leukemia."

$\mathcal{I}$F YOU WANT TO KNOW MORE ABOUT KATIE,

CHELSEA, AND LACEY,

BE SURE TO READ

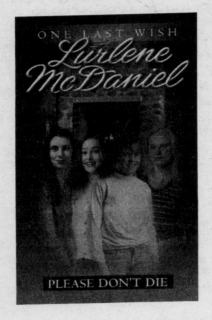

ON SALE NOW FROM BANTAM BOOKS
0-553-56262-2

Excerpt from *Please Don't Die* by Lurlene McDaniel
Copyright © 1993 by Lurlene McDaniel

Published by Bantam Doubleday Dell Books for Young Readers
a division of Random House, Inc.
1540 Broadway, New York, New York 10036

*W*hen Katie O'Roark receives an invitation from the One Last Wish Foundation to spend the summer at Jenny House, she eagerly says yes. Katie is ever grateful to JWC, the unknown person who gave her the gift that allowed her to receive a heart transplant. Now Katie is asked to be a "big sister" to others who, like her, face daunting medical problems: Amanda, a thirteen-year-old victim of leukemia; Chelsea, a fourteen-year-old candidate for a heart transplant; and Lacey, a sixteen-year-old diabetic who refuses to deal with her condition. As the summer progresses, the girls form close bonds and enjoy the chance to act "just like healthy kids." But when a crisis jeopardizes one girl's chance of fulfilling her dreams, they discover true friendship and its power to endure beyond this life.

"Me, too. I don't know what I'd do without you, Katie. Whenever I think about last summer, about how you were so close to dying . . ."

She didn't allow him to complete his sentence. "Every day is new, every morning, Josh. I'm glad I got a second chance at life. And after meeting the people here at Jenny House, after making friends with Amanda, Chelsea, and even Lacey, I want all of us to live forever."

He grinned. "Forever's a long time."

She returned his smile. "All right, then at least until we're all old and wrinkled."

$\mathcal{I}$F YOU WANT TO KNOW MORE ABOUT

KATIE AND CHELSEA, BE SURE TO READ

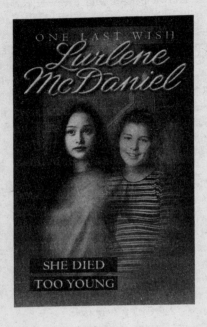

ON SALE NOW FROM BANTAM BOOKS
0-553-56263-0

Excerpt from *She Died Too Young* by Lurlene McDaniel
Copyright © 1994 by Lurlene McDaniel

Published by Bantam Doubleday Dell Books for Young Readers
a division of Random House, Inc.
1540 Broadway, New York, New York 10036

*C*helsea James and Katie O'Roark met at Jenny House and spent a wonderful summer together.

Now Chelsea and her mother are staying with Katie as Chelsea awaits news about a heart transplant. While waiting for a compatible donor, Chelsea meets Jillian, a kind, funny girl who's waiting for a heart-lung transplant. The two girls become fast friends. When Chelsea meets Jillian's brother, he awakens feelings in her she's never known before. But as her medical situation grows desperate, Chelsea finds herself in a contest for her life against her best friend. Is it fair that there's a chance for only one of them to survive?

*"Don't you see? There's one donor coming in. Only one. Who will the doctors save? Who will get the transplant?"*

*For a moment Josh stared blankly as her question sank in. "Katie, you don't know for sure there's only one donor."*

*"Yes, I do. There's only one. One heart. Two lungs. The doctor said the donor's family had given permission for all her organs to be donated." Katie's voice had risen with the tide of panic rising in her. "There's two people in need and only one heart."*

Katie and Chelsea are also featured in the novels *Please Don't Die* and *A Season for Goodbye*.

$\mathcal{I}$F YOU WANT TO KNOW MORE ABOUT LACEY,

BE SURE TO READ

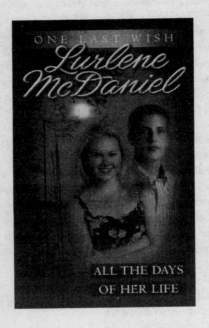

ON SALE NOW FROM BANTAM BOOKS
0-553-56264-9

Excerpt from *All the Days of Her Life* by Lurlene McDaniel
Copyright © 1994 by Lurlene McDaniel

Published by Bantam Doubleday Dell Books for Young Readers
a division of Random House, Inc.
1540 Broadway, New York, New York 10036

$O$ut of control—that's how Lacey Duval feels in almost every aspect of her life. There's nothing she can do about her parents' divorce, there's nothing she can do about the death of her young friend, there's nothing she can do about having diabetes—that's what Lacey believes.

After a special summer at Jenny House, Lacey is determined to put her problems behind her. When she returns to high school, she is driven to become a part of the in crowd. But Lacey thinks fitting in means losing weight and hiding her diabetes. She starts skipping meals and experimenting with her medication—sometimes ignoring it altogether.

Her friends from the summer caution her to face her problems before catastrophe strikes. Is it too late to stop the destructive process Lacey has set in motion?

*She went hot and cold all over. It was as if he'd shone a light into some secret part of her heart and something dark and ugly had crawled out. She had rejected Jeff because she didn't want a sick boyfriend. She'd said as much to Katie at Jenny House.*

*"It's any sickness, Jeff. It's mine too. I hate it all. I know it's not your fault, but it's not mine either."*

*"I'll bet no one at your school knows you're a diabetic."*

*She said nothing.*

*"I'm right, aren't I?"*

*"It's none of your business."*

*"You know, Lacey, you're the person who won't accept that you have a disease. Why is that?"*

*She whirled on him. "How can you ask me that when you've just admitted that girls drop you once they discover you're a bleeder? You of all people should understand why I keep my little secret."*

Lacey is also featured in the novels *Please Don't Die* and *A Season for Goodbye*.

$\mathcal{I}$F YOU WANT TO KNOW MORE ABOUT KATIE,
CHELSEA, AND LACEY, BE SURE TO READ

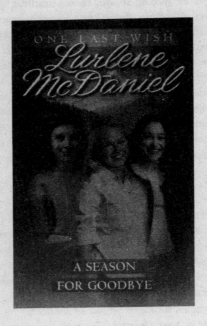

ON SALE NOW FROM BANTAM BOOKS
0-553-56265-7

Excerpt from *A Season for Goodbye* by Lurlene McDaniel
Copyright © 1995 by Lurlene McDaniel

Published by Bantam Doubleday Dell Books for Young Readers
a division of Random House, Inc.
1540 Broadway, New York, New York 10036

*T*ogether again. It's been a year since Katie O'Roark, Chelsea James, and Lacey Duval shared a special summer at Jenny House. The girls have each spent the year struggling to fit into the world of the healthy. Now they're back, this time as "big sisters" to a new group of girls who also face life-threatening illnesses.

But even as the friends strive to help their "little sisters" face the future together, they must separately confront their own expectations. Katie must decide between an old flame and an exciting scholarship far from home. Chelsea must overcome her fear of romance. And Lacey must convince the boy she loves that her feelings for him can be trusted.

When tragedy strikes Jenny House, each of the girls knows that things can never be the same. Will Lacey, Chelsea, and Katie find a way to carry on the legacy of Jenny House? Can their special friendship endure?

*"Over here!" Katie called. "I found it."*

*Chelsea and Lacey hurried to where Katie was crouched, digging through a pile of dead leaves. The tepee was partially buried, and Chelsea held her breath, hoping that the laminated photo and Jillian's diamond stud earring were still tied to it.*

*"It's come apart," Katie said, lifting up the twigs in three parts. But from the corner of one of the sticks, the laminated photo dangled, and from its center the diamond caught the afternoon sunlight.*

*The photo looked faded, but Amanda still smiled from the center of their group. Chelsea felt a lump form in her throat. These days, she and Katie and Lacey looked older, more mature, healthier too. But Amanda looked the same, her gamine smile frozen in time. And ageless.*

*Katie took the photo from Lacey's trembling fingers. "We were quite a bunch, weren't we?"*

$\mathcal{Y}$OU CAN READ MORE ABOUT

MANY OF YOUR FAVORITE CHARACTERS FROM

THE ONE LAST WISH BOOKS IN

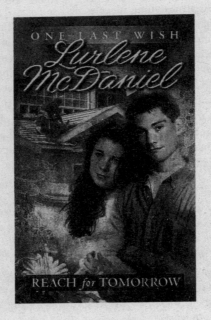

ON SALE NOW FROM BANTAM BOOKS
0-553-57109-5

Excerpt from *Reach for Tomorrow* by Lurlene McDaniel
Copyright © 1999 by Lurlene McDaniel

Published by Bantam Doubleday Dell Books for Young Readers
a division of Random House, Inc.
1540 Broadway, New York, New York 10036

$\mathcal{K}$atie O'Roark is thrilled to learn that Jenny House is being rebuilt. After the fire last year, Katie thought she could never return to the camp, where she spent the summers with young men and women like her who faced medical odds that were stacked against them. But thanks to Richard Holloway's efforts, Katie and her longtime friends Lacey and Chelsea will work as counselors once again. They'll be joined by Megan Charnell, Morgan Lancaster, and Eric Lawrence, who are newcomers to Jenny House but who have experienced the generosity of the One Last Wish Foundation.

It's not until Katie arrives at camp that she discovers that Josh Martel, her former boyfriend, is also a counselor. Katie and Josh broke up a year ago, when Katie decided to go away to college. Being near Josh again brings back a flood of old emotions for Katie. And when Josh confronts unexpected adversity, Katie knows she has to work out her feelings for him. Through the heart transplant she underwent years ago, Katie miraculously received a gift of new life. Now she must discover how to make the most of that precious gift and choose her future.

*She stopped. By now tears had filled her eyes and her heart felt as if it might break. She truly believed that God had heard her prayer. What she did not know was whether or not he would grant her request. Against great odds, God had given her a new heart when she'd desperately needed one. And he had brought Josh into her life as well. She believed that with all her heart and soul. Now there was nothing more she could do except wait. And have faith.*

*Katie lifted her arms in the moonlight in supplication to the heavens.*

# *Be my angel . . .*

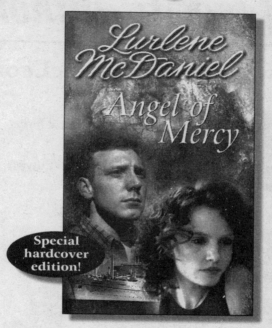

ISBN: 0-553-57145-1

*H*eather is unprepared to face the famine and misery she encounters when she joins a mission group. Only Ian, a medical volunteer, can help her see beyond the horror in this inspirational new novel from bestselling author Lurlene McDaniel.

## On sale October 1999
### wherever books are sold.

Bantam

www.lurlenemcdaniel.com

BFYR 234